THE PEMBROKESHIRE COAST
NATIONAL PARK

Herbert Williams

Webb & Bower
MICHAEL JOSEPH

Acknowledgements

My thanks to the staff of the Pembrokeshire Coast National Park, especially Deputy National Park Officer George Yeomans, Field Services Officer David Matthews and Head Ranger Malcolm Cullen; Dr Stephen Green of the National Museum of Wales; Dr Siân Rees of Cadw; Professor Gwyn Williams; Roy Mason, formerly of the Wales Tourist Board; Wendy Pettigrew of the Countryside Commission; Iona Edwards, who typed my manuscript with unfailing efficiency and patience; and my wife Dorothy, for her ever-cheerful help at all times.

All the photographs were taken for the Countryside Commission by Douglas Hardy and Gareth Davies of Archway Photography.

First published in Great Britain 1987 by
Webb & Bower (Publishers) Limited
9 Colleton Crescent, Exeter, Devon EX2 4BY
in association with Michael Joseph Limited
27 Wright's Lane, London W8 5SL
and The Countryside Commission,
John Dower House, Crescent Place,
Cheltenham, Glos GL50 3RA

Designed by Ron Pickless

Production by Nick Facer/Rob Kendrew

Illustrations by Rosamund Gendle/Ralph Stobart

Text and new photographs Copyright © The Countryside Commission
Illustrations Copyright © Webb & Bower (Publishers) Ltd

British Library Cataloguing in Publication Data
The National parks of Britain.
Pembrokeshire
1. National parks and reserves — England —
Guide-books 2. England — Description and
travel — 1971- — Guide-books.
I. Williams, Herbert
914.2'04858 SB484.G7.

ISBN 0-86350-134-6

Typeset in Great Britain by Keyspools Ltd., Golborne, Lancs.

Printed and bound in Hong Kong by Mandarin Offset.

Contents

Preface

The Pembrokeshire Coast is one of ten national parks which were established in the 1950s. These largely upland and coastal areas represent the finest landscapes in England and Wales and present us all with opportunities to savour breathtaking scenery, to take part in invigorating outdoor activities, to experience rural community life, and most importantly, to relax in peaceful surroundings.

The designation of national parks is the product of those who had the vision, more than fifty years ago, to see that ways were found to ensure that the best of our countryside should be recognized and protected, that the way of life therein should be sustained, and that public access for open-air recreation should be encouraged.

As the government planned Britain's post-war reconstruction, John Dower, architect, rambler and national park enthusiast, was asked to report on how the national park ideal adopted in other countries could work for England and Wales. An important consideration was the ownership of land within the parks. Unlike other countries where large tracts of land are in public ownership, and thus national parks can be owned by the nation, here in Britain most of the land within the national parks was, and still is, privately owned. John Dower's report was published in 1945 and its recommendations accepted. Two years later another report drafted by a committee chaired by Sir Arthur Hobhouse proposed an administrative system for the parks, and this was embodied in the National Parks and Access to the Countryside Act 1949.

This Act set up the National Parks Commission to designate national parks and advise on their administration. In 1968 the National Parks Commission became the Countryside Commission but we continue to have national responsibility for our national parks which are administered by local government, either through committees of the county councils or independent planning boards.

This guide to the landscape, settlements and natural history of the Pembrokeshire Coast National Park is one of a series on all ten parks. As well as helping the visitor appreciate the park and its attractions, the guides outline the achievements of and pressures facing the national park authorities today.

Our national parks are a vital asset, and we all have a duty to care for and conserve them. Learning about the parks and their value to us all is a crucial step in creating more awareness of the importance of the national parks so that each of us can play our part in seeing that they are protected for all to enjoy.

Sir Derek Barber
Chairman
Countryside Commission

Introduction

Long before man became urban enough to need national parks for his mental and physical health, the extreme south-west corner of Wales was noted for its exceptional beauty. To the weavers of those ancient folk tales which collectively became known as 'The Mabinogion' this was *Gwlad hud a lledrith*, the Land of Mystery and Magic.

It is easy to see why. Here the land and the sea meet as competing forces, the proud cliffs standing tall and defiant against the buffeting waves. An artist's hand appears to have been at work in sculpting rocks into strange, symbolic shapes. And inland, the moors sweep up to the brooding heights of the Preseli Hills, source of the bluestones of Stonehenge.

The mystery and the magic are still there, for those keen to feel, however fleetingly, the pulse of an ancient time. It is part of the perennial appeal of Pembrokeshire, the sense that here we are in a place apart. It results not simply from the high drama of the physical landscape, but from the social

Skokholm is famous not only for its puffins but for the beauty of its cliff scenery, the old red sandstone making an intriguing contrast with the vegetation above.

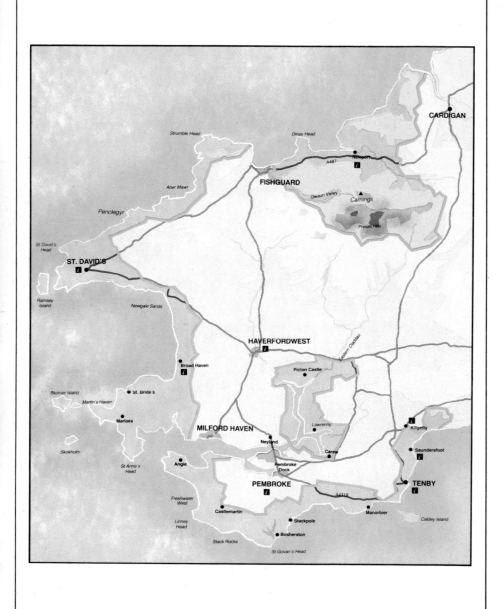

Facing. The Pembrokeshire Coast National Park.

history of a region where people of varying cultures have intermingled. Viking sea rovers gave up lives of plunder and pillage to settle here; later came the Normans, and Flemish settlers who were deliberately introduced to consolidate the conquest; and all the time the native Welsh clung stubbornly to their ancient tongue and traditions.

Like many another people who have had to give ground while still maintaining their identity, the Welsh have absorbed what were at first alien influences and woven them into the fabric of their lives. Although Pembrokeshire has been called 'Little England Beyond Wales', it is undoubtedly part of Wales. And the people living here, be they descended from Viking or Norman, Fleming or Celt, unite in declaring that it should keep its historic name, although since the local government reorganization of 1974 it has been part of the new county of Dyfed.

The Pembrokeshire Coast National Park was created in 1952. It is the smallest of the parks, covering only 225 square miles, and the only one designated primarily for its coast and seascapes. Yet while it is the sea that gives the park its special character, the hinterland – with its secret lanes, high moors and jagged cairns – has a variety which makes it almost a microcosm of the other national parks.

The coastline is, happily, within reach of everyone, thanks to the existence of the 180-mile Pembrokeshire Coast Path. With few gaps, this stretches from Amroth in the south-east to St Dogmael's in the north. You don't have to be a pack-on-the-back hiker to explore it; a stroll of only a few

Practically every turn of the Pembrokeshire Coast Path brings a new feast for the eye – here it overlooks the delightful harbour of Solva, on the north side of St Brides Bay.

hundred yards can yield timeless memories of wheeling gulls, quiet coves and headlands crowned with a wild abundance of flowers.

The cliff scenery of Pembrokeshire has a princely nobility, and the beaches vary both in texture and hue. Some dazzle the eye on a summer afternoon, whilst in the next bay the sands are as dark as the history that surrounds them. Dunes abound. And so does evidence of man's age-old struggle with the sea: quays and moorings, boats bobbing at anchor and skeleton boats long abandoned.

Pembrokeshire is famous for its off-shore islands. The very names are romantic: Skomer, Skokholm, Grassholm, Caldey. Once they provided havens for Viking raiders; now they are a refuge for huge colonies of sea birds. Grey seals breed beneath the cliffs on Ramsey Island, and they can be seen elsewhere as well. The whole park is rich in plant and animal life. Buzzards flap idly over the hills; hawks hover as they cast keen, predatory eyes about them; foxes flash across open fields. On the moors, the heather changes colour with the season, while in the country lanes spring comes early, bringing with it masses of snowdrops and celandines, primroses and bluebells. Pembrokeshire is at once prodigal and exclusive; there is even a flower called the Tenby daffodil!

The enchantment lies, however, in the unseen as well as the visible. Mystics have found these wild, rocky shores peculiarly appealing, and there were monastic communities here when Christianity in Britain was a new and potent religion. Missionaries of the Celtic Church made the perilous journey to and from Ireland in frail craft akin to the coracle, and there were strong links too with the Celts of Cornwall and Brittany. Tiny chapels near the sea dedicated to St Patrick and St Justinian bear witness to the faith and courage of these evangelists, but the crowning glory is the cathedral church of St David, or Dewi Sant, patron saint of Wales. It lies in a hollow, not through any modesty of intention on the part of its founders but because here a Christian community could be established out of sight of sea raiders. Today it has a grandeur of which David, the simplest of men, might not have approved, and some pilgrims prefer the tiny chapel of St Govan's at the foot of cliffs near Bosherston. Its very isolation speaks eloquently of the spiritual strength of the so-called Age of Faith.

Even early Christianity, however, is a comparatively late development in the life of south-

Stack rocks on the Castlemartin Peninsula, otherwise known as Elegug Stacks, is a magnet for ornithologists. Here razorbills and guillemots breed in great numbers, for this is probably the best-known auk colony in the British Isles.

west Wales. There is evidence of much older creeds, so remote in time that the beliefs themselves are lost and all we have are the outward symbols. What impetus lay behind the building of the great chambered tombs of Neolithic times? We shall probably never know, but one thing is certain: those who raised the cromlechs may have led primitive lives, by our standards of creature comforts, but they had a social organization and technology all their own. Its supreme expression is Stonehenge, which down the ages has been an object of veneration and wonder. It continues to cast a spell, even in an age which generally accords more reverence to scientific advance than religious dogma, and no-one now disputes that the bluestones of Stonehenge came from the hills of Preseli. How they got there is still a matter for intense argument, but whatever the answer, it would be a chill heart which failed to beat a little faster at the sight of those atmospheric hills. Once they stood as islands when the surrounding land was under water, and they still seem set apart, isolated not simply by their height but by something indefinable. See them on a winter afternoon, white with snow – startlingly white in the deepening gloom – and they seem to stand outside time itself. On such a day, it is easy to understand why people of ancient times may have had something of the same feeling for them as medieval man had for the cathedrals, seeing them as embodiments of faith and places sacred in themselves.

Even those who demand material evidence, rather than psychic emanations, will find plenty to ponder. As you drive along these country lanes, look out for standing stones, otherwise known as maenhirs or menhirs. Some have been turned to practical use as gateposts or boundary markers, while others stand solitary in fields or on moorland. There is a stone circle at Gors Fawr, near Mynachlog-ddu, and the Gwaun valley has a miniature Carnac, an alignment of stones of varying sizes set against a hedgebank. Some stones have assumed such significance that they have been given names – Bedd Morris, Maen Dewi – while others are in pairs, bringing to mind the 'male' and 'female' stones of Avebury.

A visit to Pembrokeshire offers different layers of experience: how deep you go is a matter of personal choice. On the surface there are the everyday sights and sounds of the villages and market towns, the clifftops with white spume below and curling gulls above, the wide beaches and secret sand dunes. It is enough for many, and no wonder. But go a little deeper, and the past becomes almost palpable. Not only the distant past of the menhirs and cromlechs, but the more accessible past of the castle builders and harbour makers. The castles at Tenby and Pembroke were assaulted by both sides in the Civil War, as they passed from Royalist to Roundhead and back again; and it was at Pembroke that Harry Tudor, the Welshman whose victory at Bosworth gave him the English Crown, first saw light of day. Only a few miles away is Manorbier Castle, birthplace of Gerald of Wales, more often known by his Latin name of Giraldus Cambrensis, who in the twelfth century travelled around Wales with an archbishop drumming up recruits for the Crusades. Gerald thought Manorbier 'the pleasantest spot in Wales', and perhaps it is even more pleasant now that the castle which symbolized the ruthless power of Norman overlords no longer threatens anyone. It stands close to the sea, and even on the briefest visit to this national park one is quickly aware that it is the sea that has shaped Pembrokeshire: not simply by ceaselessly pounding its coastline, but by providing a livelihood for its people. There was a flourishing coastal trade in the seventeenth and eighteenth centuries, when roads were so bad that the only practical way to reach this far-flung peninsula was by sea, and although the trade has disappeared the quays and slipways remain. Within living memory, Milford had one of the world's great trawler fleets; this too dwindled away, but by the 1960s the waters of the Haven, which Nelson regarded as one of the finest natural harbours he had seen, were being ploughed by supertankers making for the newly built oil installations.

This discovery of Milford Haven by the oil industry is the kind of challenge which few national parks can be expected to encounter. It reminds us that these parks do not exist in splendid isolation, insulated from change and the vulgarities of commerce, but that they are places in which people live and work. The administrators have to take note of the economic well-being of their area, which means that a plan for an oil refinery cannot be dismissed simply because such things are unlovely. They can, of course, do their best to contain the visual damage, and it's true to say that while some of the installations near Milford have actually been built within the national park, only a small part of it is affected. The search for oil and gas in the Celtic Sea

Nelson thought Milford Haven one of the finest natural harbours he had ever seen. What he would have made of the present-day supertankers is anyone's guess, but there's no doubt that the coming of the oil refineries has posed a serious challenge to the National Park.

could bring further problems, but at the time of writing these belonged strictly to the realm of speculation.

Somehow, it is only to be expected that Pembrokeshire should be a place of supertankers as well as the stones of antiquity. It is a part of Wales where contradictions flourish and opposites are reconciled. By now, the very name should be out of favour: after it was merged into the new county of Dyfed there was even a dictat that the word 'Pembrokeshire' should no longer figure in a postal address, but in the end this was no more successful than Cromwell's attempt to abolish Christmas. What stood in the way was the determination of the citizens to remain, most decisively, Pembrokeshire people. The letters continued to be delivered and, in time, one of the newly created district councils became, not simply Preseli District Council, but Preseli *Pembrokeshire* District Council. Thus does bureaucracy bow to grassroots democracy.

Since Pembrokeshire prides itself on being different, we should not be too surprised to find that this national park is divided into four distinct sections. It is hard to know when you pass from one to the other, or indeed whether you are in the park or out of it: the boundaries defy understanding. No matter. Wherever you may be, you will be surrounded by beauty and tranquillity; and who expects to find logic in a Land of Mystery and Magic?

1 The shape of yesterday

Just as a human face reflects experience, so is a landscape shaped by events. The fact that the scenery in Pembrokeshire is of infinite variety is no mere accident: it is the result of geological changes spanning millions of years.

Thus a ten-mile journey takes us from the sheer limestone cliffs near Castlemartin to the broad waterway of Milford Haven and thence to the secret creeks and shallows of the Daugleddau, the estuary formed by the meeting of two rivers. Such contrasts are to be found everywhere in this national park; only a few miles from sandy beaches and well-tilled arable land, there are rocky gorges and high moors. It is as if a huge hand had scooped up far-flung regions of the British Isles, squeezed them together and deposited them here.

From the rock-strewn summit of Garn Fawr, with its remains of an Iron Age fort, there are fine views across the open fields to the Strumble Head lighthouse.

The appearance of a landscape is determined basically by its underlying rocks, so an understanding of these and of their sequence in geological time is important. Generally speaking, the rocks in the northern part of the Pembrokeshire Coast National Park are much older than those further south. They take us back 2,000 million years, to a time when this was a region of active volcanoes: Mynydd Carningli, which overlooks the ancient borough of Newport, consists of this very hard igneous rock.

When the volcanic eruptions ceased, the sea advanced, due to a sinking of the earth's crust. It was then that the Cambrian rocks were formed out of huge deposits of sediment on the sea bed. The sandy, gritty layers are particularly well displayed in the cliffs between St David's and Newgale, and on

A geological map of Pembrokeshire showing how, as a general rule, the rocks in the north tend to be much older than those in the south.

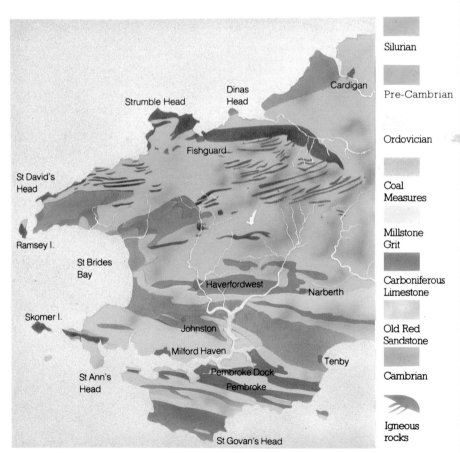

Silurian

Pre-Cambrian

Ordovician

Coal Measures

Millstone Grit

Carboniferous Limestone

Old Red Sandstone

Cambrian

Igneous rocks

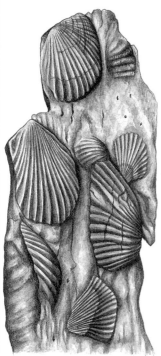

the south shore of Whitesand Bay. It was a sea alive with creatures we can study today as fossils: water fleas and sponges, trilobites and brachiopods. The trilobite is a distant ancestor of the lobster and crab, and fossilized remains a foot in length have been found in Solva harbour.

The volcanoes beneath the sea became active again, throwing out lava which accumulated in layers thousands of feet thick. This was in Ordovician times, 450 million years ago. The volcanic rock known as rhyolite, a light-coloured lava, can be seen on the Preseli Hills, and the cliffs at Strumble Head consist of lavas dating from this period. Sills of dark-coloured dolerite, formed when molten rock was forced into the sediments, have given us some of Pembrokeshire's most striking headlands – Penclegyr, Penllechwen and St David's Head – and the jagged ridges near St David's known as Carn Llidi and Penberi.

In Silurian times, warm coral seas stretched over southern Britain, nurturing marine creatures which included primitive types of sea urchin. Rocks from this period, formed from shallow-water marine sediments, are found in abundance around Haverfordwest and along the banks of the Western Cleddau. At Marloes and Wooltack some of the beds are unusually rich in coral. Further north, an outcrop follows the north coast from the Teifi estuary to Newport Bay and Dinas Head, but in general Silurian rocks are less exposed than Ordovician.

Towards the end of the Silurian period, 400 million years ago, the geography of Pembrokeshire changed dramatically. The land was forced up by

The brachiopod, similar to the cockle, was one of the most common invertebrates living in the Devonian period, 350 million to 400 million years ago. The remains of creatures like this went into the making of the carboniferous limestone cliffs of south Pembrokeshire.

Carn Llidi, on St David's Head, stands out from afar. At one time, though, it was part of a high plateau which has, for the most part, been eroded away. From the top one can see, on a clear day, the mountains of Snowdonia and the Wicklow Hills of Ireland.

intense pressure from within, and mountains appeared where, for nearly 200 million years, there had been only sea. These mountains stretched all the way from southern Britain to northern Scandinavia, across the Old Red Sandstone Continent. The first vertebrates appeared – heavily armoured, fish-like ostracoderms, swimming in estuaries and rivers. Corals and sponges were numerous, trilobites in decline. The pounding rain eroded the land, and with the slow accumulation of pebbles and sand, deltas and swamps were created. In northern Britain, the great range of the Caledonian Mountains reached into what is now the Atlantic, and the Preseli Hills are all that is left of the mountains that once stood there. They have been worn down to their present size by the slow erosion of rain, wind and ice, the bite of frost and the churning of many rivers. The pressure exerted on rocks that once formed the ocean bed was so intense that as they were thrust up to great heights they folded and cracked, and the complex geological pattern that resulted is splendidly revealed in the steep cliff faces along the north shore of St Bride's Bay, between St David's Head and Newgale Sands. Look out, too, for narrow outcrops of Silurian rocks between Haverfordwest and Whitland.

If we could climb aboard a time machine and see the Pembrokeshire that existed then, how strange it would seem! Wide rivers flowed through the mountains, and for months on end the sun beat down. Then came the rainy season, as abrupt and dramatic as in tropical countries today. Strange fishes swam in the warm seas, but there were also more familiar forms of life, such as snails and mussels. Rain spots appear in some of the old rocks of Pembrokeshire, proving the general aridity of the climate. Others are marked by ripples or have been cracked by ancient suns. Note, too, the reddish hue of many cliffs, further evidence of a climate arid enough to allow the oxidization of iron minerals.

Some of the uppermost beds of rock in the outcrops south of Milford Haven – notably at West Angle, Freshwater West, Stackpole, Caldey and Skrinkle – suggest that though the mountains rose to the north, this area was covered by a shallow sea. The fossils match those in Devon dating from this Devonian period, and they mark the first incursions of a sea in which the succeeding limestones were to be laid down.

The carboniferous limestone cliffs of the Castlemartin peninsula are rich in fossilized corals, which speak of a time when the climate was equatorial and giant ferns grew in swamps and lagoons.

The reddish tint of some of the Pembrokeshire cliffs bear witness to the changes that have taken place in the climate. They tell us that millions of years ago it was far more arid than today, causing chemical changes that have left a permanent mark on the landscape.

It was a sea abounding in life. There were brachiopods and crinoids – related, respectively, to cockles and starfish – and colonies of corals. Seaweeds, of a kind secreting a limy skeleton, carpeted the sea floor with growths resembling biscuits or buttons. Between the sea and the mountains of north Pembrokeshire there were swamps and lagoons nurturing luxuriant vegetation, such as giant ferns and club mosses, and the climate was equatorial.

The Carboniferous Limestone rocks of south Pembrokeshire are almost entirely composed of the skeletal debris of marine organisms. The purity of some of the beds, virtually free of extraneous sand and mud, indicates clear, shallow waters. Strange to think that it was on that ancient sea floor that the high cliffs of the Angle peninsula had their genesis – tiny shell upon shell, bone upon bone, until today we have these headlands rising 250 feet above sea level. The stretch of coast between Stackpole Head and Linney Head is a particularly fine example of this process. The cliffs are rich in fossils, and so are many of the inland quarries.

In Upper Carboniferous times the land rose again to the north, and the faster-flowing rivers washed a vast amount of sand and mud down to the coast. Plants died and peat beds formed, and in time the peat was compressed into seams of coal. Thus were the foundations laid for coalfields which, while small in scale, flourished in the nineteenth century and continued until after the Second World War, the last pit closing in 1947. Beneath the Coal Measures are bands of Millstone Grit, which can be seen as a sequence of folded and puckered shales on the foreshore of Tenby North Sands. The Coal Measures are clearly exposed each side of Saundersfoot between Monkstone Point and Amroth, and along the coast of St Bride's Bay from Talbenny to Newgale. The lower beds are predominantly shaly and contain the anthracite coal seams; the upper beds include thick sandstone. Fossilized plants appear in some of the shales.

Look out for red marls and sandstones along the southern stretch of coast between Tenby to the east and Linney Head to the west, notably in the Lydstep Skrinkle cliffs and in Bullslaughter Bay, three miles west of St Govan's Head. They belong to Triassic times, 200 million years ago, when the climate was hot and arid, as in the Sahara today. The red marl was formed when the dust raised by storms became trapped in the stretches of salty water that made a variation in the parched, monotonous landscape. Pembrokeshire, and indeed the whole of Britain, was then part of a huge land mass and the nearest sea was in central Europe.

The underlying rocks of Pembrokeshire are fractured and folded, yet much of its surface consists of a fairly smooth plateau with deeply incised valleys. Why is this? The answer is that the plateau,

Sunset at Amroth. The smooth sands enshrine the past; sometimes, at very low tide or after a storm, the matted remains of a prehistoric forest are revealed.

Glen Beach at Saundersfoot is on one of the most sheltered shores of the national park. From the coastal path on nearby cliffs there are fine views south-east to Rhossili Down, at the tip of the Gower Peninsula.

out of which the Preseli Hills rise so dramatically, was once an old sea bed. It was not raised all at once but in a series of pulses, which explains why there are distinct 'steps' in the plateau. The rain beating down on it over countless centuries created rivers, which cut through the surface to form those little valleys so typical of Pembrokeshire. No wonder the country lanes plunge and rise so abruptly!

Once we know this, light is thrown on other mysteries. Why that Ridgeway between Tenby and Pembroke, an arching spine bristling like a miniature version of the Hog's Back in Surrey? Why Penberi and Carn Llidi near St David's, isolated heights overlooking a plain? These are, in fact, survivors: in times long gone they did not stand out at all, but were part of other steps in the plateau which have, for the most part, been eroded away

Even a very limited knowledge of geology enables us to see things we would otherwise have missed, and view the whole landscape in a new and exciting way. Look out in Porth Clais for that phenomenon known as a 'raised beach'. It's a peep into the past, for this wave-cut platform above the present sea level indicates the line the beach took during one of the warm intervals, or interglacials, in the Ice Age. The melting of the ice sheets meant a rise in sea level, which dropped again as the climate became colder. These raised beaches are thus above the present high-water mark. There are other raised beaches at Freshwater West, Manorbier Bay, Swanlake Bay, West Angle Bay and on Caldey Island.

Again, the coast between Strumble Head and Caerbwdi shows how the shape of a landscape is

The sandy beach at West Angle is a good place for viewing tankers passing in and out of Milford Haven. The nearby cliffs have interesting geological formations.

determined by the strength or weakness of its underlying rocks. Bays are formed when rocks crumble away beneath the ceaseless onslaught of the sea, whereas harder rocks stand up to the attack to give us those headlands of grit, sandstone or igneous rock.

Towards the end of the Tertiary period, about two million years ago, the British Isles were beginning to assume their present shape. The climate was sub-tropical, and in the warm seas sharks and corals thrived. Then came the first signs of the encroaching Arctic cold. Ice sheets and glaciers spread far south over Britain, and ever since then, periods of intense cold have alternated with warmer interglacial times.

In Pembrokeshire, the landscape bears few signs of any intense glacial erosion, but ice-scratched rock surfaces are to be found at 500 ft (152 m) on Carn Llidi and in Whitesand Bay, south of St David's Head. The glaciers deposited erratic boulders here and there: some are scattered across Craig Talfynydd, a mile north-west of Mynachlog-ddu. A moraine of ice-scratched stones is to be found at the lower end of Foel Cwmcerwyn, just east of the Pantmaenog Forest near Rosebush, probably dating from the time of the last glaciation, a 'mere' 17,000 years ago!

The carns on the eastern side of Mynydd Preseli

There are superb seascapes at Whitesand Bay, where the Atlantic rollers provide fine surfing for the adventurous. It was from here, legend has it, that St Patrick set sail for Ireland.

One effect of climate on landscape can be seen on the eastern side of Mynydd Preseli: the jagged carns of frost-shattered rocks which stand out boldly against the sky.

show the destructive properties of frost, which shattered the bedrock during the period when the ground was frozen solid most of the year. One of the best examples is Carnmenyn, the jagged outline of which can be seen from the unclassified road between Mynachlog-ddu and Crymych. Nearby are other carns or tors, including Carnalw and Carn Goedog. Carn Arthur, half a mile due west of Carnmenyn, has a boulder balanced, apparently miraculously, on two upright rocks, and another point of interest here is the boulder stream in the hollow between Carnmenyn and Carn Arthur.

The existence of granite pebbles in the boulder clay of Pembrokeshire is further evidence of the movement of ice. They match pebbles in Arran, Ailsa Craig and Galloway in Scotland, and on the Isle of Man. Thus we can infer that the ice sheet covering the region had its origins far to the north in the Clyde estuary and the Irish Sea. Very large 'erratic' boulders are scattered over southern Pembrokeshire – one from Scotland lies in the village of Bosherston, while another from North Wales overhangs the extremity of St Govan's Head. Some of the deposits contain shells of mussels, cockles, whelks and periwinkles, which were dredged from the sea floor as the ice moved in from the north-west.

The slow melting of the glaciers as the Ice Age came to an end caused radical changes in the Pembrokeshire landscape. The Gwaun valley which runs east from Lower Town, Fishguard, was cut by the surging meltwater of the Irish Sea glacier. One theory has it that this glacier still thrust into the coast long after the local ice had disappeared, preventing the free flow of rivers into Cardigan Bay and St George's Channel and damming up glacial lakes in the river valleys along the north and west coasts. It was believed that the Gwaun valley, and narrower valleys running into it, were formed by overflow from the lakes, but more recent opinion is that they were gouged out by meltwater flowing under the ice. This later theory is based on the discovery that the meltwater must have been flowing uphill for many miles, which it could only do if it were contained in a geological structure resembling a pipe and subjected to intense pressure. These valleys today are places of serene beauty, with wooded slopes and peat floors: the most accessible include the Criney valley and Esgyrn Bottom, west of Llanychaer.

In the same area, the appearance on the map of

'islands' which are surrounded by land is explained by the fact that that at one time they were cut off from the mainland by spillways. Barry Island (Ynys Barri), between Abereiddy and Porthgain, is one; Dinas Island, of which Dinas Head is the most northerly point, is another. At the western end of Milford Haven, Dale Roads provided the exit for a spillway from St Bride's Haven, three miles to the north, and the Wooltack peninsula and the Neck of Skomer were isolated by overflow channels. The Treffgarne gorge, five miles north of Haverfordwest on the Fishguard road, was cut by meltwater rushing south towards Milford Haven, and the Haven itself is the most dramatic relic of the last retreat of the ice between 12,000 and 15,000 years ago. Twenty-four miles long and a mile and a quarter wide at its mouth, it was formed when glacial ice melted to drown what had once been a broad valley threaded by a meandering river. Before the ice, sea level was at least one hundred feet lower than at present, but during an earlier interglacial it stood higher, creating cliffs and narrow rock-cut benches along both shores. The Haven is considered a classic example of a ria – that is, a river valley flooded by a rise in sea level – and Solva harbour is a smaller-scale example.

One of the gems of the National Park is Solva, where the pleasure boats bob on translucent waters. Do not be deceived into thinking that life here has always been leisurely; once there was a thriving coastal trade and ruins of lime kilns remain.

There are tales of lost kingdoms under the sea around all the coasts of west Wales, and although the stories are pure romance they are based on a solid core of truth. There was a time when the land did reach out much further than today; when people grazed their flocks on pastures which now lie fathoms deep beneath the waves. Sometimes the curtain is drawn back; a very low tide, or the shifting of the sands by a storm, reveals traces of submerged forests at Wiseman's Bridge, Amroth, Manorbier, Newgale and elsewhere. These tangled, matted remains are a strangely moving sight, reminding us of the profound changes that can take place in an environment, even in a period of time which, geologically speaking, is no more than the blink of an eye.

2 The cromlech makers

In Tenby Museum there are simple tools that take us back 12,000 years, to the time when Pembrokeshire was a wasteland racked by cruel winds and roamed by reindeer. They prove that this harsh landscape, with its steppe vegetation, was inhabited not only by creatures which have long since been extinct in Britain, such as the giant ox, but by a species which has proved far more adaptable: man.

There are caves in south Pembrokeshire which have yielded scrapers and gravers, scattered among the bones of the animals stalked by the hunters who from time to time lived in these primitive shelters. Little Hoyle Cave near Tenby, otherwise known as Longbury Bank, was explored in 1866 by the Reverend HH Winwood, who discovered a variety of bones there, including those of domesticated animals such as goats and dogs. Nearly a century later, Professor Charles McBurney found, at a depth of eighteen inches to two feet, 'a thin scatter of bones and rare lumps of charcoal, and a single typical large Creswellian type pen-knife blade'. He also produced evidence of reindeer, bear and fox, and in 1984 Dr Stephen Green discovered that in the late glacial times arctic hare had lived in the region, as well as collared and Norway lemmings. Professor McBurney concluded

In prehistoric times there were flourishing communities on Skomer Island, and hut circles like this show us the bare outline of the past, leaving the imagination free to weave what fancies it will. There are traces of old field patterns, too.

that 'the environmental and chronometric evidence demonstrates that the surviving cave deposits at Little Hoyle span some 50,000 years at least'. Bones have also been found in Hoyle's Mouth Cave, near Tenby, and excavations of Priory Farm (Catshole quarry) Cave, near Pembroke, and Nanna's Cave on Caldey Island have produced objects which no less an authority than Dr W F Grimes has described as 'a kind of pen-knife' which 'links these Pembrokeshire hunters directly with their contemporaries elsewhere in Britain as possessors of the Creswellian culture, so named from the caves at Creswell Crags in Derbyshire, where more clearly than anywhere else it could be seen that the cave-dwellers of Britain had developed differently from their contemporaries in south-western France and elsewhere on the Continent'.

In post-glacial times, from around 8000 BC onwards, there was a trend towards more open settlement, and Mesolithic people built flimsy shelters where they assiduously chipped away to make flint barbs and blades which they then ingeniously mounted in wood, bone or antler shafts. Thus were harpoons and other weapons fashioned. Armed with these, they set out to hunt and fish in the forests and marshes. It is in this period, too, that the first archery in north-west Europe is known to have been practised.

The places where these hardy ancestors of ours lived are now known as flint chipping-floors – their work is remembered, their domesticity forgotten – and the coastal lands of Pembrokeshire have yielded many examples of these. The sites include Nab Head, St Bride's; Small Ord Point, Caldey; Little Furzenip, Castlemartin; and Swanlake, Manorbier. Some of the old hunting grounds now lie beneath the waves, as at one time the land reached out much further than it does today and Britain was joined to the Continent. Around 6500 BC, however, it became an island and by the end of the Mesolithic era, around 4000 BC, sea level was much the same as it is now.

After the hunters came the farmers of Neolithic times, the first people to till Pembrokeshire soil. The first agriculturalists must have arrived by sea, and their ideas were absorbed by the people already living in south-west Wales. The adoption of techniques such as the breeding of stock and the growing of wheat and barley enabled a more settled life to be lived than ever before, and with this increased sophistication came the development

The cliffs at Abercastle overlook Cwm Badau, the Valley of Boats, first mentioned in the sixteenth century as a safe harbour. The Carreg Samson cromlech is at nearby Longhouse.

of crafts such as pottery. There was, too, a steady improvement in skills which earlier generations had possessed. It became customary to grind stone axes, thus making them sharper and more effective, and they were produced in such numbers that archeologists refer to axe 'factories', a curiously modern term for a prehistoric activity. There are believed to have been two 'factories' on the Preseli Hills, although the actual sites have not been found. The raw material in one of them was the spotted dolerite which provided the most distinctive of the 'foreign' stones of Stonehenge, while the other dealt in silicified tuff, a rock likely to have come from the eastern end of the range. Axes from both these centres are widely distributed, showing that these Neolithic people had a social organization not to be despised.

Bronze Age axe-heads like this show how, around 2000 BC, increasingly sophisticated tools and weapons were being manufactured in Britain. Swords, shields, chisels, sickles and cooking pots of bronze have been found in many parts of Wales.

One of the most important New Stone Age sites in Pembrokeshire is Clegyr Boia, a mile west of St David's. This tump – which in geological terms ranks as a monadnock, the remnant of a mountain standing above an eroded plain – owes its name to Boia, an Irish freebooter who is reputed to have lived there in later times. Remains of simple huts have been found, as well as stone axes and round-bottomed bowls similar to those dug up in Ireland and Cornwall. The most impressive artefacts of Neolithic man, however, are the great stone tombs we call cromlechs or dolmens. There are splendid examples of these in north Pembrokeshire, notably Pentre Ifan, four miles south-east of Newport. A roadside signpost points the way to it, and a short path provides easy access. At any time of year it is impressive, but in winter twilight it is peculiarly haunting, framing Mynydd Carningli within its

The gaunt remains of the Pentre Ifan burial chamber have a haunting beauty. What we see here is the entry to the chamber, the whole of which was covered in earth. It was raised by the Neolithic people who inhabited this region about 5,000 years ago.

upright boulders and capstone. Raising this portal was an engineering feat which would pose a challenge even today, and only the most unimaginative could fail to be awestruck in its presence. It reminds us of the immense skill which ancient man possessed in transporting large stones and erecting huge monuments. The capstone at Pentre Ifan is sixteen and a half feet long, weighs at least as many tons and is supported at a height of seven and a half feet by three uprights. Such burial chambers were originally covered by earth mounds or barrows, and at Pentre Ifan the outline of the mound is visible.

Building these monuments was clearly a task of such magnitude that the ritual of burying the dead

With a combination of simple technology and brute force, the cromlech makers managed to shift large stones and raise them into position.

must have had great importance in Neolithic times, but when the culture died so did reverence for the dusty remains within these slowly disintegrating tombs. For centuries, sites like Pentre Ifan received little respect from people living in the vicinity, who understandably plundered them for their stone or whatever else they could put to good use. By the time Pentre Ifan was subjected to anything like a scientific scrutiny, virtually all traces of the burials had vanished, although there were fragments of pots linking this cromlech with a series of tombs in Ireland.

The ruined chamber at Garne Turne, two and a half miles east of Wolf's Castle on the south side of Preseli, is of a similar type to Pentre Ifan, and other long-cairned tombs are related to it, although lacking the distinctive portal and façade. Their chambers are usually oblong or box-like, and there is sometimes more than one chamber in the same mound. A cromlech on the hillside near Trellyffnant, north of Nevern, appears to have two chambers, and so does the dolmen at St Edrins, near Solva.

The cromlechs with polygonal as opposed to oblong chambers are known as passage graves, because they were entered by way of the round mounds which enclosed them. The finest example is Longhouse, just off the country lane between Trevine and Abercastle. It has a large capstone supported by a number of uprights, but no trace of the mound remains.

Further south, not far from Neyland, the Hanging Stone between the villages of Burton and Sardis has a passage which owes its survival to its incorporation in a fieldbank, which has both concealed and protected it.

On a coastline exposed to fierce winter gales, Abercastle has always been a safe haven for seamen. In summer it makes a picturesque scene, with a variety of small craft casting reflections on the tranquil waters.

The third main series of dolmens are distinguished less by their form than by their association with igneous outcrops between St David's Head and Goodwick. They have simple chambers with capstones supported either on low uprights or on natural ledges in the surrounding rocks. They appear to have been covered by cairns rather than earth, and must have looked like small, artificial caves. Most are in ruins now, and are hard to find in high summer because of the surrounding bracken. The best example is probably Garnwnda, just outside the hamlet of Llanwnda between Goodwick and Strumble Head, but there is also King's Quoit on the headland at Manorbier, where the capstone has been drawn forward by the collapse of its outer uprights.

Even the wisest of us knows but little about the cromlech makers, and the society in which these megaliths had both a practical and a symbolic purpose. Archaeologists sift the dust, and make what they can of the scanty remains they find. One fondly held set of beliefs gives way to another, and the assumptions of one generation are despised by the next. If we are humble enough to confess it, we know little more than those ancients who, long after the culture which produced the cromlechs had withered and died, believed them to be the work of legendary heroes such as King Arthur of the Round Table. There is a Carreg Coetan Arthur at Newport and another Coetan Arthur on St David's Head, while the Longhouse dolmen is known locally as Carreg Samson – though which Samson this may be is anyone's guess. Even into the nineteenth century, antiquarians were still insisting that the capstones were altars on which druids made human sacrifices:

Carreg Samson at Longhouse, near Abercastle, is one of the cromlechs in Pembrokeshire bearing names of legendary heroes.

the mystery surrounding them is such that they invite romantic, even lurid, explanation.

The most intriguing mystery of all is the precise link between Stonehenge and Pembrokeshire. Ever since the discovery that the Stonehenge circles are partly made up of bluestones which could only have come from the Preseli Hills, argument has raged over how they come to be there. The distance between Salisbury Plain and Preseli is around 120 miles as the crow flies, but since even Neolithic crows could scarcely have been much help in transporting these huge boulders, each weighing up to four tons, the actual journey involved must have been much longer – probably 180 miles or more. The theory which finds most favour with archaeologists, although this may change in years to come, is that the bluestones were taken to Stonehenge by a variety of methods. Wherever possible they would have been placed on rafts and transported along rivers, the Bristol Channel providing a more serious challenge to the navigational skills of those charged with the task. Where there was no alternative to moving them by land, people would have been engaged on the back-breaking task of hauling them on sledges,

At any time of year, the Preseli Hills have a haunting beauty. They can be seen from afar, and there is much speculation about the place they held in the scheme of things for prehistoric man. It was from this region that the bluestones of Stonehenge came.

under which rollers might have been placed.

So much for the conventional view. There are others. One is that the bluestones were carried all that way not by human effort but by sheer accident. It was the great Irish Sea glacier, so this theory goes, that picked up the bluestones on Mynydd Preseli and deposited them on the fringe of Salisbury Plain, where many centuries later they were happily seized on by the Wessex builders of megalithic monuments. Those who dismiss this notion contend that there is no glacial evidence to support it, but the final word has not been said on the matter – and, given the distance in time when the events in question took place and the disputatious nature of archaeologists, it probably never will be. The most fanciful theory of all proposes levitation as the answer. The priestly builders of Stonehenge, it is suggested, had the power to raise the stones off the ground by a kind of thought process and direct them to Salisbury Plain. This has even less support than the glacial theory, yet legends of 'walking stones' persist in many parts of the world: the Easter Island figures, nine feet tall and weighing up to fifty tons, are said to have moved themselves under the orders of a chieftain with supernatural powers.

Whatever the answer, it is easy to see why, for Neolithic man, the Preseli range may have had a mystic significance. Even today these hills have an eerie quality about them. Overlooking the plateau, they seem much higher than they are, and driving through them at dusk they appear remote and inaccessible, cut off from our mechanistic civilization by a certain timelessness. If they can arouse this feeling in twentieth-century man, what power did they hold for the ancients?

There is nothing to compare in size with Stonehenge in Pembrokeshire, but an interesting stone circle can be seen just off a well-surfaced minor road skirting Mynydd Preseli. Gors Fawr stands on the moorland three-quarters of a mile west of the village of Mynachlog-ddu. A sign indicates its position only one hundred yards or so from the road. It is one of the monuments listed by Aubrey Burl in his comprehensive work, *The Stone Circles of the British Isles*. Burl makes the point that it is graded towards the south-south-west, 'a custom that seems to have become popular in the mid-second millenium in Southern Britain'. Behind the circle rises Mynydd Preseli, its bare slopes scattered with the rocks that have lain there since the ice departed. Look to the right, where two

The well-defined stone circle of Gors Fawr had been likened to a giant sundial, with outlying stones giving an alignment on the midsummer sunrise over nearby Foel-drych. It is near the village of Mynachlog-ddu.

upright stones stand in a field over 200 yards away: they are unlikely to be so close to the circle by accident. The circle has been likened to a gigantic sundial, and it is also suggested that the outlying stones contain their own axial alignment on the midsummer sunrise over the nearby Foel-drych hilltop.

A cairn circle exists a few miles further west of Mynachlog-ddu at Dyffryn, just south of the Rosebush Reservoir. This consists of a ring of upright stones enclosing a round barrow, and is of a type rare in this part of Wales. Standing stones, on the other hand, are commonplace; a list drawn up early in the 1970s showed no fewer than seventy of them in Pembrokeshire, mainly in the north. The compilers of the list carefully excluded anything of dubious origin, such as cattle rubbing stones.

One of the most curious collections of stones in the national park is at Parc y Meirw, near Llanychaer, in the picturesque Gwaun valley. This alignment is easily missed if you aren't looking out for it, yet it has a fascination for those who linger awhile. The stones are of various sizes, and some suffer visually through being embedded in a hedgebank, but when the mists swirl around them it is easy to be filled with the sense of mystery and awe one feels amid the alignments at Carnac in Brittany. In scale Parc y Meirw bears no comparison with that colossal assembly, yet size has little to do with instinctive reactions of this kind. Turn right by the pub in Llanychaer, take the first turning right and, after about a mile, look out for the alignment on the right-hand side of the road, just past a cattle grid.

Pairs of stones are more frequent than groupings, and since the tendency is for one stone to be slight

Bedd Morris (Morris's Grave) stands on the moorland above Newport. The name may owe more to the fertile imagination of people living in the vicinity long after the stone had been placed there than to historical fact. It is one of seventy standing stones in Pembrokeshire.

and tapering and the other more substantial, they are thought to be sexually symbolic: the 'male' and 'female' stones at Avebury come into this category. In Pembrokeshire, two good examples of this kind of pairing are to be found in the vicinity of the stone circle at Gors Fawr: Cerrig Meibion Arthur and the Waun Lwyd stones above Dolaumaen.

Some of the stones which stand alone may once have served as waymarks on ancient tracks, while others are like massive gravestones, marking burial places. It is uncertain, however, which came first, the stone or the burial. One school of thought has it that people were buried there simply because the stones themselves were idols or cult objects. Evidence of elaborate rituals was found when the stone on the slopes of Rhos y Clegyrn, a mile east of St Nicholas, was excavated.

The names of these single stones can be deceptive. It seems clear, at first glance, that Bedd Morris (Morris's Grave) marks a burial place, but what we must remember is that it was given this name in comparatively modern times, so that it bears no relationship to the stone's original function. It is easy to see why fanciful stories should be woven around these strange, isolated boulders, as they

The beautiful Gwaun valley provides this interesting stone alignment at Parc y Meirw (Field of the Dead). It is in a region of the National Park rich in standing stones and ancient associations.

often stand in romantic situations: Bedd Morris is high on the moors above Newport, with the craggy summit of Mynydd Carningli rising to the east. Conveniently for the traveller, it stands by the roadside, and so does Maen Dewi on Dowrog Moors near St David's. There are also Harold stones to be found, supposedly marking the site of victories over the Welsh by Harold, Earl of Wessex, whose brief rule as King of England ended at Hastings in 1066.

Most of the standing stones and circles belong to the Bronze Age rather than Neolithic times, although to think of a sharp distinction between the two is misleading: cultures merge, and there is a transitional stage spanning centuries. The metal workers of the Bronze Age came to Pembrokeshire about 2500 BC and are known as Beaker folk, after the distinctive pots they manufactured. They were enterprising traders, importing copper axes from Ireland, but like Neolithic people are best remembered for their ways of disposing of their dead. They buried them in round barrows of earth, or round cairns – often placing the body in a stone box, known as a cist. The burial places tended to be conspicuously sited on hilltops or ridges, where they were silhouetted against the sky. Clearly, for the Beaker folk the dead had abiding importance. They often placed beakers and daggers beside the bodies, which suggests a belief that the dead could carry such objects into an after-life. Barrows and cairns break the Preseli skyline in many places. The three largest Bronze Age cairns are on the top of Foel Drygarn, 1,190 ft (360 m) above sea level, and there are others on Freni Fawr, Foel Feddau, Foel Cwmcerwyn, Foel Eryr, Mynydd Cilciffeth and Mynydd Castlebythe. Smaller cairns stand on the flanks of some carns such as Carnbica.

It may seem strange that these memorials should have been raised in such remote places, if they were intended to act on the imagination of the living, but we must remember that at the time people tended to live on the lower slopes of hills, rather than in the lowlands: river valleys were often thickly wooded. Even today there are hill paths which follow the line of ancient tracks where travellers would have passed quite close to the barrows and cairns. One such is Flemings Way, which crosses the main Preseli ridge: the name is deceptive, since the track existed long before the first Fleming set foot in Wales. (It has also been called Roman Road, Pilgrim's Way and, more luridly, Robber's Road.) Treading it now, free as air, we feel we have left the

▲	Cave
●	Neolithic occupied site
◢	Burial chamber
●	Round barrow
●	Medieval occupied site
⛩	Cromlech
●	Earthworks
▮	Standing stones
✝	Early Christian stone

Some of the historical sites to be found in Pembrokeshire.

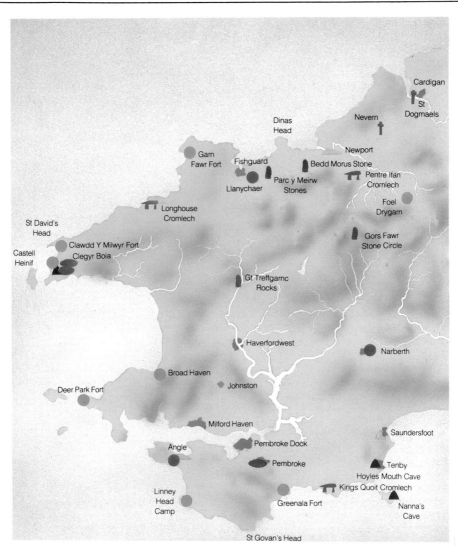

Cardigan

St Dogmaels

Nevern

Dinas Head

Newport

Garn Fawr Fort

Fishguard

Bedd Morus Stone

Pentre Ifan Cromlech

Parc y Meirw Stones

Llanychaer

Foel Drygarn

Longhouse Cromlech

St David's Head

Clawdd Y Milwyr Fort

Gors Fawr Stone Circle

Castell Heinif

Clegyr Boia

Gt Treffgarnc Rocks

Haverfordwest

Narberth

Broad Haven

Johnston

Deer Park Fort

Milford Haven

Saundersfoot

Angle

Pembroke Dock

Pembroke

Tenby

Hoyles Mouth Cave

Kings Quoit Cromlech

Linney Head Camp

Greenala Fort

Nanna's Cave

St Govan's Head

busy world behind: yet in Bronze Age times this was a trade route, a vital link with Ireland and the gold of the Wicklow Hills. The Ridgeway running west of Tenby to Angle, in south Pembrokeshire, follows another ancient track. On the Ordnance Survey map it appears to run only between Tenby and Lamphey, but this is deceptive: beyond Pembroke the B4320 to Angle follows the line of the Ridgeway, which passes groups of barrows at Dry Burrows and Wallaston. Barrows are termed 'tumuli' on the Ordnance Survey map, and over the centuries those

on hilltops have been given the name of Beacon or
Bigney. Thus we have Corston Beacon on the Angle
peninsula and, further north, Llanrhian 'Bigney'
near Trevine. Interestingly, the appearance on the
six-inch Ordnance Survey map of the house name
'The Beaconing'near Steynton, just outside Milford
Haven, led to the discovery of a round barrow in a
nearby field.

At Corston Beacon a man was found to have been
buried with a bronze dagger, and the excavation of
a small cairn on Linney Burrows, near Castlemartin,
revealed a crouched skeleton with a crude pot
beside it. This reminds us that, while Neolithic
people had favoured communal burial in chamber
tombs, by Bronze Age times individual burial had
become customary. Around 1500 BC the fashion
changed again: bodies were cremated and the
charred bones buried in a pit, or placed in an urn.

Some barrows have been used for successive
burials over a span of many centuries. Kilpaison
Burrows, on the Angle peninsula, is one of these.
After the first cremation the ashes were put in a pit
in the centre of the barrow, but the sanctity
surrounding this ancient tomb meant that in the
course of time it was used for further burials,
possibly hundreds of years after the first ceremony.
The discovery of a skeleton in a stone-lined grave of
AD 500 or 600 tells us that the mound was in use as a
burial ground for fully 2,000 years.

About 600 BC, bronze gave way to iron as the
dominant metal, and the centuries leading up to the
arrival of the Romans saw the incursion into the
region of Celts. It is no longer fashionable to think in
terms of their arrival *en masse*, the cautious
archaeologists of today preferring to imagine a
constant trickle across the English Channel and the
North Sea. What is more or less certain is that during
these centuries the fortified settlements known in
Pembrokeshire as promontory forts or 'raths' came
into existence. They consisted of a cunning
arrangement of banks and ditches which remain in a
debased form even now, and huts which have long
disappeared. Here on sea cliffs, and hill summits
inland, these small, resolute communities passed on
their traditions and skills from one generation to
another.

One of the best examples of a fortified cliff site is
to be found at St David's Head, in a position of wild
beauty. Clawdd-y-Milwyr, the Warrior's Dyke, has
a massive inner rampart with the remains of
drystone walling. Within the rampart there were

The rugged coastline of St David's Head is notable not only for its wild beauty but for its fortified settlements dating from Bronze Age times. Offshore is Ramsey Island, separated from the mainland by the swirling waters of Ramsey Sound.

circular huts, traces of which can be seen. This once formed a compact settlement on a rocky headland where the view takes in Ramsey Island and, farther out to sea, the scattering of rocks known as Bishops and Clerks. East of the rampart, the boundary of the settlement is defined by the ruined wall drawn obliquely across the promontory. Even more fascinating, perhaps, is the evidence of a field system dating back to Iron Age times. This can be seen beyond the wall, on the slopes of the valley between Porthmelgan and Carn Llidi. Precise dating is impossible, but it was probably farmed in two distinct periods, the walls separating the rows being put there in the later phase. The smaller fields belonging to the original inhabitants of this windswept settlement are now covered by the undergrowth on the south side of the valley, and are difficult to recognize. They serve to remind us that the people of Clawdd-y-Milwyr practised a mixed economy, rearing stock, cultivating the land, going fishing, and eating sea birds' eggs as well as the birds themselves. They were also weavers: weights from their looms are on display in Tenby Museum.

Clawdd-y-Milwyr is inaccessible by car, but can be reached along the coastal path. The complex as a whole gives us a good picture of an Iron Age settlement with its strong defences encircling the domestic area, and the outlying fields: a self-reliant community which had to be capable of surviving not only the vagaries of weather but the assaults of its enemies.

The most southerly coast of the national park has a series of well-defined promontory forts between Linney Head and Greenala Point, east of Stackpole

Quay. Some of this is in the Castlemartin firing range, where access is restricted. Greenala is an elaborate site with surprisingly powerful earthworks for a comparatively small area. Fishponds camp at Bosherston is a much larger site which was apparently occupied three to four centuries before Christ. Strategically its position was even stronger then than it is today, as the valleys it overlooks were at that time open to the sea, making it a convenient landing place as well as affording protection against invaders. Two forts on the Dale/Marloes peninsula – Deer Park, west of Marloes, and Great Castle Head, near St Ishmael's – had similar virtues. The Linney Head camp near Castlemartin was at first a simple structure with a single line of defence, but later it was given a double row of ramparts, traces of which are still visible. The nearby tank ranges remind us that, unhappily, mankind has not become less war-like in the intervening centuries.

The word 'rath', which is applied to many of these sites, is unusual in Wales. It comes from Ireland, where it describes a different kind of prehistoric fortification. Confusingly, in parts of Pembrokeshire one sometimes comes across a so-called 'rath' which is in fact a medieval motte-and-bailey castle, but in the national park itself the raths are genuine Iron Age promontory forts, relying partly on the natural strength of their position for their defence. Some were still in use in the Romano-British period and, like the Bronze Age barrows, they attracted 'developers' who came hundreds of years after the original builders: one was found to be occupied in the first century BC and again in the second century

The rocky crags of Garn Fawr hillfort provided natural protection.

AD. In addition to Clawdd-y-Milwyr, St David's Head has other well-preserved raths at Porth y Rhaw, west of Solva; Castell Heinif, overlooking Ramsey Sound; and Penpleidiau, which straddles the promontory between Caerfai Bay and Caer Bwdy Bay and has no fewer than four defensive banks.

In north Pembrokeshire, the word 'rath' gives way to the Welsh 'castell' (castle). Look out on the Ordnance Survey map for the name Castell Coch (Red Castle): there is one alongside the coastal path at Aberdinas, another on the Pen Castell Coch headland north of Trevine, and a third at Penmorfa, where the outer bank has a field wall, possibly dating from the eighteenth century, built on top of it.

The coastal promontory fort has its counterpart inland in the hillforts, the best example of which is Foel Drygarn. Here, on the eastern edge of the main Preseli range, the Iron Age settlers built a complex stronghold which encloses three Bronze Age burial cairns. Steep crags gave natural protection to the west and south, but to the east and north double stone ramparts and ditches were constructed, making this a seemingly impregnable stronghold. The number of hut hollows and platforms suggest that it was well populated, and we begin to visualize these long-ago people a little more clearly when we look at their spindle whorls, beads and stone lamps in Tenby Museum.

Another hillfort of outstanding interest is on the summit of Mynydd Carningli. Here, at a height of 1,100 ft (330 m), these hardy folk hacked a series of enclosures out of the hard, volcanic rock and felt safe enough at some stage to put huts outside the defences as well as within them. The hut sites are still visible, the most accessible being on the western slopes.

The third site of special importance is Garn Fawr, which stands near the coast south of Strumble Head. Again, rocky crags provided natural protection, but elsewhere on the site deep ditches were dug, and banks of earth were faced with drystone walls.

Carnalw, just over a mile west of the summit of Foel Drygarn, provides an example of a defensive work rare in Britain: chevaux-de-frise, a set of low, pointed stones set at an angle in the ground to deter an attacking force. It had its equivalent in Wales in the Second World War, when iron stakes were driven into the ground in some coastal areas as tank traps. The idea for the chevaux-de-frise may have come from northern Spain, where hillforts with

concentric defences are common, and there are only half a dozen other examples of this wickedly ingenious device in the whole of the British Isles. Carnalw is, however, accessible only to hardy hill climbers, who should bear in mind always that even on an apparently settled, sunny day mists can descend suddenly to turn a friendly environment into a hostile one.

The pretty village of Moylegrove, on the road from Newport to St Dogmaels, was named after Matilda, wife of Robert Martin, Lord of Cemais. Cargoes of lime were once discharged at Ceibwr Bay, a mile away.

The Great Treffgarne rocks, west of the main road between Haverfordwest and Fishguard, catch the eye much more easily: standing high above the gorge of the Western Cleddau, they look like grotesques from the hand of a crazed sculptor. The hillfort here has bank-and-ditch defences, and an outwork guarding the entrance. There are hut circles just outside the protected area, and traces of early fields.

When changing modes of life led to the abandonment of such sites, those on high ground were vulnerable to the depredations of time, but less likely to be spoiled by man than the fortifications in more accessible places. There are earthworks in relatively low-lying areas which have been extensively ploughed for many generations, and it is hard now to distinguish them as ancient sites. Four miles north of Milford Haven, however, there is an Iron Age fortification still recognizable as such, in spite of its alteration by farming. This is the deceptively named Romans Castle, south of the unclassified road between Tiers Cross and Walwyn's Castle. The ramparts of the main enclosure are well preserved and still impressive, but additional defences on the western and southern sides of the fort have been flattened or taken into the modern fieldbanks. Caerau Gaer, near the village of Llanddewi Velfrey, is equally vulnerable; part of its outworks have been absorbed into the road-bank. Close by is Llanddewi Gaer, which can be classed by design as a promontory fort, although nowhere near the sea. To the south-west, in the Castlemartin peninsula, there is a miniature hillfort half a mile north of Merrion and another – in the military zone – on the slopes of Buliber Down.

Some of the Pembrokeshire Iron Age forts are on the slopes of hills, rather than their summits. Thus we find Summerton camp, just above a disused quarry a mile or so west of Puncheston, a good example of a concentric defensive work. There is a similar site at Caerau near Moylegrove, which lies in the northern part of the national park by the minor road between Newport and St Dogmaels. Scollock rath, on the fringe of the Llys-y-fran Country Park, is interesting for its resemblance to Helsbury fort in Cornwall, and the similarity between the chevaux-de-frise on Carnalw and some of the defensive works in Spain, taken with pottery and other finds of the same period, shows that people separated by great distances had close cultural links.

The fortified sites provide the boldest examples of Iron Age occupation, but a study of the countryside has also revealed 'open' settlements in which people lived in their round, thatched huts close to the fields they tilled. Like the hillforts, they demonstrate how the people of ancient times took readily to locations now thought remote and uninhabitable. The island of Skomer was covered with fields, and there were settlements on the slopes of the Preseli hills. It requires a vivid imagination to picture these deserted places as busy communities, inhabited not by woad-covered savages but by people whose feelings were much the same as our own, facing the harshness and uncertainty of life as best they could, creating an inner core of domesticity out of chaos. Our imaginations are helped, perhaps, by a visit to the replica of a thatched Iron Age round house at Castell Henllys, just off the A487 trunk road between Newport and Cardigan. It is in our hearts, however, that we must make the sympathetic leap to try to see the world through their eyes, as they went about their day-to-day concerns in a landscape which, geologically, was much the same as it is now.

3 Sea rovers and saints

When the Romans came to Wales, they considered the people of the south-western peninsula homogeneous enough to be known, collectively, as the Demetae: the name from which that of the present-day county of Dyfed is derived. To the east was the tribe they called the Silures, while mid-Wales was occupied by the Ordovices.

These tribes were often engaged in bitter warfare with each other, though capable of uniting in a common cause. To what extent they united against the Romans, if at all, is not known: the certainty is that the invaders built a fort at Carmarthen, which they called Maridunum. In Pembrokeshire itself, evidence of the occupation is scanty. There are sites of Roman character, but nothing military in design. This may argue complaisance on the part of the Demetae or, alternatively, that the Romans did not think it worth their while to extend their influence further west; or perhaps something of both.

The site of a so-called 'villa' appears half a mile to the west of the main Haverfordwest–Fishguard road, near Wolf's Castle. It stands about 200 yards east of a small earthwork known as 'Roman camp' on many older maps, and as 'Settlement' on more recent ones. Chance discoveries made in 1806 leave no doubt that this was a building with Roman characteristics and sporadic finds since then appear to confirm this. The site is hard to find, especially in summer, when it is overgrown. Better known, perhaps, is that of the oddly named Castle Flemish, which early antiquarians called Ad Vigessimum. On the most recent Ordnance Survey map this is not accorded the dignity of either name, but simply exists as a 'settlement' straddling the country lane that runs east of Wolf's Castle to join the B4329 south-west of Tufton. It consists of a rectangular bank and ditch, and appears to have been occupied in the late first and second centuries AD. Traces of wooden buildings were found during excavations, but the long-held view that it was a military outpost is now discounted: it is more likely to have been a defended farmhouse. So too, was a stone building which stood on a hilltop looking out to sea north-

St Govan's Chapel, near Bosherston, speaks of the time when some felt that the only way to lead a holy life was to seek places of wild seclusion. The chapel, reached by a flight of steps, was built on the site of a hermitage of the Dark Ages.

west of Amroth: it is known to archaeologists as Trelissy, but again, appears on the map as a settlement. There are probably similar sites waiting to be discovered, and until more information is obtained it is hard to see how they fit into the pattern of Roman occupation in the area.

The departure of the Romans early in the fifth century meant the loss of the coastal patrols which protected the Demetae against sea raiders from Ireland. Later came the Vikings, still a by-word for terror. These were the so-called Dark Ages, which nevertheless saw the establishment of Christianity in place of paganism. Strange to think that Patrick, patron saint of Ireland, may well have been born in Wales near the spot where St David's Cathedral now stands. The more zealous converts went to remote places to devote themselves to prayer and contemplation; discomfort was joyfully embraced.

One hermit chose to live in a cleft in the rocks at the foot of a cliff near Bosherton; later, St Govan's Chapel was built there, and today it can be visited by descending a steep flight of steps. Legends abound. Some say the empty bellcote once held a silver bell which was stolen by pirates, whose boat was wrecked as soon as they put to sea; the bell was returned by sea-nymphs, and now lies entombed in a rock. Another story concerns the steps; if you count them going down, it is claimed, when you come up they make a different number. A well beyond the door in the south-west corner reputedly had healing powers, but discreetly ran dry in the twentieth century; whether in deference to modern medicine, or in protest against the spirit of the age, is uncertain. Another well is still to be seen inside the building, and this too is said to have healing properties, especially for those suffering from diseases of the eye; it was found when the chapel was restored. Most of the building dates from the thirteenth century, but the cell cut out of the rock, and the altar and bench, are of much earlier origin; perhaps they go back to the fifth century when, it is said, the quest for holiness first began here.

St Govan's was one of many small, isolated chapels built around the coast of Pembrokeshire. Mostly they are in ruin now; some are obscured by wild, tangled briars, while others still raise rickety walls to the winds. They were places where sailors offered prayers before and after voyages, and were dedicated to saints of the Celtic Church, which for centuries developed along its own lines, cut off from the Church of Rome. Its ritual, as well as its organization, differed in important respects from that of Rome, and many centuries were to pass

Many cathedrals dominate the landscape for miles around, but this can't be said of St David's. It is placed, curiously, in a hollow – curious, that is, until one realises that it stands on the site of an older Christian settlement cunningly shielded from the eyes of Viking raiders.

before it became absorbed – reluctantly – into the Roman Catholic Church. The names of men once revered now often have only topographical relevance, but one still stands out: that of St David, patron saint of Wales. Although many places claim him, one theory is that he was born near the site of the ruined chapel dedicated to his mother, St Non, on a clifftop just outside St David's. An abstemious man, he neither ate meat nor took strong drink, and has come to be called Dewi Ddyfrwr, David the Water-Drinker – Dewi being a Welsh form of David. He was also strong in resisting other, possibly greater, allurements, for when the pagan Irish chieftain, Boia, tempted David and his monks with the sight of naked women prancing around, David is said to have remained true to his monastic vows. On the site of the sixth-century community he founded on the banks of the River Alun, St David's Cathedral now stands, and has, among its treasures, superbly carved choir stalls from the late fifteenth century and a roof of Irish bog oak.

There are no buildings dating from the earliest period of Christianity in Britain, but inscribed and carved stones of religious significance do survive. Some of these bear the curious script known as ogham, which originated in Ireland and is further evidence of the common Celtic culture which united the lands around the Irish Sea in the so-called Dark Ages. There was, in fact, a heavy migration of people from Ireland into south-west Wales towards the end of the Roman period. The immigrants belonged to the Deisi tribe of southern Ireland and apparently moved in under Roman patronage. The earliest ogham stones go back to the fifth century, but the most striking of all, the great stone cross in Nevern churchyard, dates from the tenth or eleventh centuries. Intricately carved on all four sides, it stands in the shade of a yew tree, a monument to craftsmanship as well as faith. The church and cross commemorate St Brynach, and legend has it that every year on the saint's feast day, April 7, the first cuckoo to return to Pembrokeshire used to perch on the cross. Mass would not begin until it arrived, but one year it had such an exhausting journey that it turned up late and instantly dropped dead. Comfortingly, we are told that we may either believe this tale or disbelieve, 'without peril of damnation'.

Nevern church, which is exquisitely set beside a stream in tranquil countryside, has other relics of the remote past: two stones with inscriptions in both

The stone cross beside Nevern Church is a remarkable sight. Dating from the tenth or eleventh centuries, it is exquisitely carved. An earlier cross carved in Latin and Ogham is in the church porch.

Latin and ogham. Other examples of ogham script can be found in the churches at Brawdy, Bridell (on the A478 south of Cardigan), Caldey and Steynton, near Milford Haven.

The Nevern stone cross has counterparts at Carew and Penally. The Carew cross stands at the roadside in the village, and was reputedly raised around 1035 in memory of Maredudd ap Edwin, a descendant of the great law-maker Hywel Dda (Howell the Good). In all there are no fewer than 120 stones in Pembrokeshire which can be associated with the first centuries of Christianity in Britain, and while many have been placed in churches – and in St David's Cathedral – for safe keeping, others are still out in the open, and are even in use here and there as gateposts.

The Vikings had little respect for Christian stones of any kind, and are believed to have ravaged St David's eight times in the centuries leading up to the Norman Conquest. In the winter of 877, a chieftain called Hubba (who gave his name to Hubberston) sheltered in Milford Haven with a fleet of twenty-three ships and 2,000 warriors. In time the Vikings found it more profitable to make quick killings of a different kind, and came to these shores as traders rather than warriors. Curiously, the only archaeological evidence for all this activity is a small lead object, probably a weight, with a Norse dragon set in brass. It was found on the shore at Freshwater West and is now in the National Museum of Wales in Cardiff. Viking influence is strong, however, in the place names of Pembrokeshire: Skokholm, Grassholm, Skomer, Goodwick, Gosker, Goultrop all speak of the days of the Scandinavian sea rovers. There are also similarities between blood groups found in south Pembrokeshire and those of Scandinavia.

The Normans left more obvious marks of their presence. The first to arrive were the warriors of Roger de Montgomery, who had been created Earl of Shrewsbury only five years after the Conquest. They came from the direction of Cardigan, overrunning the old Welsh administrative divisions of Emlyn and Cemaes, Penbro and Rhos. The lands were conferred on Earl Roger's younger son, Arnulf de Montgomery, whose 'slender fortress of stakes and turf' at Pembroke passed to Gerald de Windsor and became, in time, the formidable stone castle which still dominates the town. The Normans had the power to conquer by force of arms where necessary, and the cunning to exploit differences

Skokholm is a name of Scandinavian origin. The island provided a refuge for the sea rovers whose superb seamanship enabled them to take their longboats to the most unpromising shores.

Giraldus Cambrensis called it 'the pleasantest spot in Wales' – Manorbier. He was born in this castle in the twelfth century and left a memorable account of a journey through Wales.

among the Welsh princes. A castle was built in a strategic position at Haverfordwest, eighty feet above the River Cleddau, and other fortresses took shape at Roch, Wiston, Llawhaden, Narberth and Amroth. These defined the limit of the invaders' strength: although they had a presence north of this line, their real power lay to the south. Thus we find the origin of the Landsker, the imaginary line separating the Welsh-speaking north of the region from the 'English' south.

The social effects of the Norman occupation were far-reaching, as it meant the introduction of feudal methods of land tenure, farming on a larger scale, and a Church organized on diocesan lines. It also meant the establishment of towns, which grew around castles. These Marcher lords gathered immense power to themselves, and were in effect petty kings, with their own courts to administer what they regarded as 'justice' and stinking dungeons into which the unruly were flung. Within the town walls the freemen known as burgesses had a monopoly of trade. Castle, manor and borough formed the 'Englishry' of the lordship; the 'Welshry' lay outside.

One of the most impressive castles was built at

Manorbier, in a narrow valley – then wooded – a few hundred yards from the sea. This was the seat of the de Barri family, who if they never did anything else justified their existence by giving us Gerald de Barri, otherwise known as Giraldus Cambrensis. This quirky figure was a keen observer of the social scene, a man who today would be perfectly at home in the world of the colour supplement or television studio. He was born, as near as we can tell, in 1146, and left us a marvellous account of a journey through Wales in the company of an archbishop who was acting as a kind of recruiting officer for the Crusaders. He paints a vivid picture of a frugal people making do with one good meal a day, and living in huts built out of tree branches twisted cunningly together. They rubbed their teeth with green hazel till they were ivory-white, and unlike the English – who were deferential towards their social superiors – they weren't afraid to speak out boldly in the presence of their chieftains. The men were 'light and active, hardy rather than strong' and 'dared to attack an armed foe' even when unarmed themselves. Their staple diet consisted of milk, cheese, oats and butter, and they tended to eat more meat than bread. Have the Welsh changed much in 800 years? Giraldus describes a volatile people with a love of argument, poetry and music, little taste for commerce and a fine ear for harmony: 'They do not sing in unison like the inhabitants of other countries,' he observes, 'but in many different parts.' So what's new?

Not all the castles built by the Normans were on the scale of Manorbier and Pembroke. Some were much simpler strongholds consisting of a conical mound or motte flanked by a bailey (enclosure) containing the living quarters, stables and stores. Alternatively, instead of raising a mound, a large area was surrounded by a bank and a deep ditch; this was known as a ringwork. Surmounted by evil-looking palisades of pointed stakes, and defended by ruthless warriors, they must once have been fearsome sights, but now they blend into the landscape like natural growths. It's fun trying to trace the outline beneath the nettles and brambles. Look out for earthworks half a mile west of St David's at Parcycastell in Merry Vale, and further north, Castell Nanhyfer or Nevern Castle – which stands above the church – is a Norman stronghold which may well occupy the site of an earlier, Iron Age hillfort. The same applies to Walwyn's Castle, south of the B4327 between Haverfordwest and

One of the attractions of Tenby is the variety of its seascapes. Not far from the smooth open sands so deservedly popular with visitors are the North Cliffs, and Goscar Rock.

Dale. Such earthworks are more plentiful than the grander ruins of those frowning stone fortresses; they account for more than thirty of the fifty castles raised in Pembrokeshire by the Normans. In such compact, well-made strongholds they looked out over a landscape where many peoples had already passed, adding yet another chapter to the story of man's abiding ambition and violence.

The stone castles stand close to the sea or tidal water, and some replaced earlier fortresses of the Welsh. At Tenby, a 'fine fortress above the ninth wave' was eulogized by a ninth-century bard enjoying the hospitality of the court of Bleiddedd ab Erbin, a prince of the ancient kingdom of Dyfed. The Normans raised their own fine fortress on this rocky headland, though little of it remains. Hard to believe now that much blood was spilt on this tranquil spot: that the sons of Gruffydd ap Rhyd marched across the sands from Amroth and slew the garrison in 1153, that Maelgwyn ap Rhys brought further slaughter in 1187, and that the great Welsh warrior-prince Llewelyn the Last sacked the town in 1260. Tenby owes its present street plan to the rebuilding that followed Llewelyn's assault, although now only one of its five gates remain. Almost all the town wall, however, is intact.

The Welsh name for Tenby is Dinbych-y-Pysgod – the little fort of the fishes – and even to the most

unmilitary of eyes the strategic value of its position is obvious. So, too, is that of the once great castle of Haverfordwest, which stands on a spur above the Western Cleddau at the lowest fording point on the river. The castle was founded around 1100 by Gilbert de Clare, Earl of Pembroke, who made good use of the lie of the land: nature provided ready-made defences around most of the perimeter, and a powerful curtain wall, twelve feet thick in places, dampened the spirits of even the most ardent attackers.

In the north on the old county boundary with Cardiganshire, Cilgerran Castle invited attack by the Welsh when it stood for foreign oppression, and the attention of landscape painters when it declined into graceful ruin. Still an inspiration to romantics, the ivy-clad ruins, much restored, stand in rural tranquillity above the River Teifi.

Like Cilgerran, Carew Castle has tested the vocabularies of writers aspiring to lyrical heights. It overlooks a tidal creek in the lower reaches of the Daugleddau, a seductive and somewhat mysterious region of the national park. Once it was the fortress home of Sir Nicholas de Carew, but like other castles which remained in occupation rather than

Reflections on the water . . . and the ivy-covered walls of Carew Castle inspire other kinds of reflections, too. It was built as a bastion of security in troubled times, but later became a symbol of opulence.

falling into picturesque ruin, it was extensively modified by owners who in more settled times were able to give luxury precedence over impregnability. Sir Rhys ap Thomas held a famous tournament there in 1507, to celebrate the knighthood bestowed on him by Henry VII, the Welshman he had helped to raise to the throne. Half a century later Sir John Perrot, reputedly the natural son of Henry VIII, built the great Elizabethan block with its large mullioned windows, and he even gave the castle a piped water supply. Today the National Park Authority has a ninety-nine year lease of the castle and forty acres surrounding it, including the tidal mill – generally known as the French mill – which is the only one of its kind still surviving in Wales. Its first appearance in any written records was in 1541, and it continued to grind corn up to 1937. Castle and mill are both open to the public, and guided walks are available.

Pembroke Castle is best known as the birthplace of Harry Tudor, who ascended the English throne after landing on the Dale peninsula and marching to Bosworth. Traditionally he first saw light of day in the tower now named after him, to the left of the entrance as one approaches the castle. The Great Keep in the inner ward is one of the finest of its kind in Britain, and by the Monkton Tower one can still see the Water Port, through which the water supply was brought in by earthenware pipes. Beneath the castle is a natural cavern in the limestone rock. This is known as the Wogan, and was used as a boathouse by the garrison.

The Normans brought changes to the religious as well as the secular life of Wales. The old Welsh Church, a branch of the Celtic Church, lost its independence and with it the ancient customs to which it had steadfastly clung – for instance, priests were allowed to marry. The country was now divided into dioceses presided over by bishops, and sub-divided into parishes served by priests. (The Welsh Church had been non-territorial in nature.) A new kind of monastery appeared: not one which, as in the old days, was simply a centre for missionary endeavour, but a place of retreat from the world. The Welsh naturally regarded the new foundations with suspicion; they seemed a symbol not so much of redemption as of foreign domination. The first to appear were the Benedictine priories, which were generously endowed by the Marcher lords with grants of land and other gifts. One of these was at Monkton, near Pembroke; originally

The French mill at Carew, like the castle nearby, is leased by the National Park Authority. These two historic buildings, overlooking a creek of exquisite beauty, are on the fringe of the mysterious Daugleddau region.

Every day in the summer boatloads of tourists go to Caldey Island, where the community of monks uphold the age-old Cistercian tradition of industriousness by farming the island and making perfume.

this was a cell of the abbey of Seez in Normandy, which shows the closeness of the bond between these religious houses and the Continent. Some of its remains, including a dovecote, now form part of Priory Farm, but its sanctuary has been incorporated into the parish church. In the north, St Dogmael's belonged to the Reformed Benedictines, and the north and west walls of the nave still stand almost to their full height; look out for the beautiful ball-flower moulding on the north door and the figures of an angel, a lion and the Archangel Michael in what remains of the north transept. At one time there were two monasteries in Haverfordwest, one a priory and the other a friary; only the scanty ruins of a cruciform church belonging to the priory can now be seen, adjoining Freeman's Way. Questions of faith aside, the fact that so much craftsmanship could be destroyed so arbitrarily at the time of the Dissolution of the monasteries is a wry commentary on the fragility of human endeavour. Caldey, however, shows how an ancient tradition can be restored, after an interval of many centuries. The first monks to go there belonged to the Celtic Church, for Caldey was then Ynys Pyr, Pyr's Island – Pyr being the abbot, who is said to have drowned by falling into a well in a drunken stupor, a scurrilous legend possibly encouraged by the Benedictines, who went there in the twelfth century. After Henry VIII closed down the monasteries and shared their wealth among his friends the island was given over to farming and limestone quarrying until 1906, when a community of Benedictines built the present priory. It was

The towering walls of the Bishop's Palace at St David's give us an insight into another age, when high officers of the Church were key figures in the government of the realm. The medieval bishops who lived here took important administrative decisions.

transferred to the Cistercians in 1929 and raised to an abbey in 1958. Caldey is now a tourist attraction, with regular boat trips from Tenby. The perfume made by the monks has a steady sale. The Cistercians have always been noted for their diligence – in medieval Wales they were great breeders of sheep and they now run a successful farm on Caldey.

Priories and friaries apart, there is another class of ecclesiastical building in Pembrokeshire giving us an insight into the medieval mind: the bishop's palace. It seems odd to us now that at a time when most of the people around them were living in grinding poverty, bishops should be so ostentatiously comfortable, but no doubt there are inconsistencies in our own thinking for which future generations will take us to task. The huge palace next to St David's Cathedral rivals any castle for its curtain walls and battlements: evidently even bishops felt the need to be protected by something more physical than faith. At Lamphey, two miles east of Pembroke, the bishop's palace reached heights of luxury in the fourteenth century which made it fit for a king: there were fishponds, orchards, a herd of sixty deer and every comfort the times could provide. The ruins of another bishop's castle are to be found at Llawhaden. It was built to protect the estates of the bishops of St David's, and stood on a high ridge overlooking the Eastern Cleddau.

When the hatred between Norman and Welsh was still intense, King Henry I decided to teach the natives a lesson by putting even more foreigners in their midst. These were the Flemings who had arrived as refugees in his realm, after giving up the fight against constant floods in their homeland on the Flanders coast. He sent many of them to settle in Pembrokeshire, where they added a new strain to the already mixed population. They proved to be hard-working and adaptable, manufacturing cloth and trading with the Continent; some became seamen. Before long Flemings were taking over manors and even castles, and their endowments helped the Church to prosper and expand. Politically they were allied with the Normans against the Welsh, who were a constant threat. Thus came the division of Pembrokeshire into south and north, a division by language, custom and sympathy which has helped to give the county its unique flavour. When the killing stopped the Welsh remained in the north, tenaciously farming thin, grudging soil which would have broken the hearts of some of their southern neighbours. In the south – the area known as 'Little England Beyond Wales' – different attitudes prevailed. The dividing line between north and south became known as the Landsker, a word with Viking origins. South of the line, new

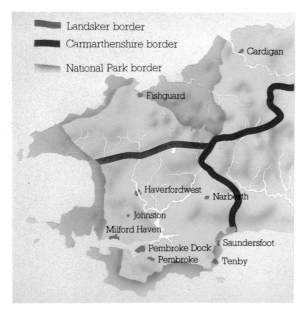

Landsker border
Carmarthenshire border
National Park border

Cardigan
Fishguard
Haverfordwest
Narberth
Johnston
Milford Haven
Pembroke Dock
Saundersfoot
Pembroke
Tenby

The Landsker is the imaginary line showing the linguistic division in Pembrokeshire between the north, where Welsh speakers tend to be concentrated, and the more anglicised south – 'Little England beyond Wales'.

The round chimneys known as 'Flemish chimneys' still survive here and there, although they have long outlived their original function. They date from the fifteenth and sixteenth centuries, when some of the techniques employed earlier in raising the castles were being transferred to domestic architecture.

settlements were established with such names as Hayscastle, Slebech and Rudbaxton. The way of life was English, with farms and cottages around a castle or fortified manor house. There were open fields with strip cultivation, and moorland with common grazing rights. The churches had high towers with battlements, which in the early days served as watchtowers against Welsh raiders. The 'Flemish chimney' began to make its appearance, tall and round and peculiar to Pembrokeshire if not peculiarly Flemish. In short, this was an area where the colonizers made their own distinctive imprint on the land. Five centuries after their arrival, the antiquarian George Owen remarked that 'a stranger travelling from England and having ridden four score miles and more in Wales . . . and coming hither to Pembrokeshire . . . would imagine he had travelled through Wales and come into England again'. The diet was 'as the English people use . . . beef, mutton, pig, lamb, veal and kid, which usually the poorest husbandman doth daily feed on'. The 'upper part of the shire' or Welshry, however, was 'inhabited with Welshmen, the first known owners of the country', such as were 'never removed by any conquest or stranger'. He defined these as 'the people of the hundreds of Cemais, Cilgerran, Dewisland and part of Narberth', where there were 'gentlemen that to this day do hold and keep their

St Issells church in Saundersfoot is a picture of tranquillity now, but its fortified tower served as a lookout in the days of conflict between anglicised south Pembrokeshire and the Welsh-speaking north.

ancient houses and descent from their ancestors for 400, 500, 600 years and more'.

The difference between north and south can still be observed. The churches of the north, with bellcotes rather than towers, make an interesting contrast with those in the south. Again, examples of the Welsh longhouse are still to be found in the countryside north of the Landsker; originally the living rooms were at one end of the building and the byre at the other, the intervening space being used as a cattle-feeding walk. We no longer find people being ostracized for marrying 'across the line', yet it is still in the north that Welsh tends to be spoken, while the people of the south have an accent akin to that of the West Country. Visually, the linguistic distinction between north and south has been blurred by the adoption of bilingual place-names throughout Pembrokeshire by Dyfed County Council. These have now been generally accepted, although there was a feeling at first that the scholars advising the highways department had been hard put to find authentic Welsh names for some of the villages in the south.

The surnames of Pembrokeshire make an interesting study. Someone called Gibby, Gambold, Skyrme or Lowless clearly belonged south of the Landsker in days of old, but time has brought about some strange ironies. The genealogist Francis Jones has pointed out that there are Welsh-speaking families in the north with Norman names like Martell, Miles, Mortimer, Devereaux and Reynish, while in the south there are monoglot English speakers called Griffith, Howell, Craddock, Bowen and Rees.

It is equally true that people on either side of the Landsker have contributed to one of Pembrokeshire's strongest traditions: that of seafaring. We find its beginnings in the Middle Ages, when the Anglo-Norman planned towns of Haverfordwest, Pembroke and Tenby developed a trade with the Continent as well as with the ports of the Bristol Channel. Wine and salt came in from France and timber, fresh fruit and spices from Spain and Portugal, while the exports were of grain, cattle, wool, skins and hides. At first glance it seems odd that an inland town like Haverfordwest should have grown into a port long before Milford Haven, but it had the advantage of standing on a tidal river, and even in medieval times its mayor bore the proud title of Admiral of the Port – a title which survives to this day. In contrast Milford, although

Some of the old lime kilns at Solva – relics of a busy past. This picturesque coastal village, an artist's dream, has a long seafaring tradition. Its peak years as a port came midway through the nineteenth century, but now it has a new role as a centre for sailing dinghy enthusiasts and cruiser owners.

occupying a prime position on a waterway which Nelson described as one of the greatest natural harbours in the world, had to await the vision of some early town planners at the close of the eighteenth century.

Whatever the long-term effects on Welsh social and cultural life, Henry VIII's Act of Union of 1536, uniting England and Wales politically, served to give a further impetus to trade. Dale and Angle, on either side of the entrance to the Haven, grew into busy small ports, and vessels called regularly into Popton, Hubberston and Pwllcrochan. In the north, Fishguard was particularly busy in the herring season, and Newport had built up a lucrative trade with Bristol by Elizabethan times. Oysters, now a luxury, were a part of the working man's diet then, and a typical cargo of 20,000 went from Pembrokeshire to Barnstaple in 1592. The trade went into decline in the latter part of the nineteenth century but is now reviving, and several oyster farms have been set up in recent years.

The remains of lime kilns in many of the small harbours of Pembrokeshire remind us that even in medieval times, the beneficial effects of spreading lime on acid soils like these were recognized. The limestone generally came from the southern part of the county, and was exposed to the fierce heat of the kilns for several days. The lime was then cooled and taken in carts to the fields where, as George Owen noted in Tudor times, 'it destroyeth the furze, fern, heath and other like shrubs growing on the land, and bringeth forth a fine and sweet grass and quite changeth the hue and face of the ground'.

There were less reputable trades in old Pembrokeshire. In the seventeenth and eighteenth centuries, the local magistrates not only turned a blind eye to smuggling but had a hand in it themselves. There were pirates too, notably Bartholomew Roberts, from Little Newcastle, whose one claim to virtue is that he drank nothing stronger than tea. Black Bart was the terror of the Spanish Main, and is said to have captured 400 ships. There were wreckers in Pembrokeshire too, hanging out false lights to lure ships on to the rocks. Bodies washed ashore were stripped of their rings and the wrecks were ruthlessly plundered by people who endured desperate poverty: it is much easier to be moral with money in the bank.

Meanwhile, the face of the countryside was changing. The old communal system of open-field farming could not survive in an age when wealthy people were growing wealthier still by enclosing common land without let or hindrance. Remarkably, it is still possible to discern strip fields on the medieval pattern around the villages of Angle, Cosheston and Letterston. Before the enclosures, no fewer than 3,000 young people in the county were employed in herding cattle from the age of ten, George Owen remarking that they were so tanned by exposure to all weathers that 'they seem more like tawny Moors than people of this land'. The cattle included Castlemartin blacks, which the drovers took in great herds to Smithfield market in London. Traces of the old drovers' roads can still be seen on Mynydd Preseli, but it is hard for us now to picture a world in which travel was so difficult that most people rarely ventured from the parish in which they were born.

Naturally, it has always been easier to farm the low-lying southern parts of Pembrokeshire than the northern uplands, and even in medieval times the peninsulas of Castlemartin, Dale and St David's were yielding bumper cereal crops. Owen observed that wheat from the hundred of Castlemartin 'maketh the bread fairer than any other wheat of the shire', and that he had not seen better land for growing corn than that around St David's. He also noted that cattle were bred in all parts of the shire, but they were mostly to be found 'in the Welsh parts and near the mountains'.

The struggle with nature was arduous enough without the conflicts between powerful rivals which from time to time stained the fields with blood. The Civil War between King and Parliament in the seventeenth century brought sorrow to many a Pembrokeshire household. The issue was complicated by the fact that some powerful figures in the local community showed no compunction in changing sides, sometimes at the most peculiar times. When the Royalist cause was all but lost the mayor of Pembroke, John Poyer, switched his allegiance from Parliament to King, bringing on his head the wrath of Cromwell, who forced the surrender of the castle after a seven-week siege. There was also a siege of Tenby Castle, which in the course of the war was bombarded from the sea by both sides.

More than a century later, during the American War of Independence, there was a curious incident involving the buccaneering John Paul Jones, who sailed into Fishguard Bay, seized a merchant ship and demanded a 500-guinea ransom. When it was refused he fired two broadsides on Lower Fishguard, injuring the sister of the author Richard Fenton. Worse was to follow in 1797, when the French sent an invading army to these shores. The history books record it as the Last Invasion of Britain, although it never posed a serious threat to the realm. It came about when the French decided that Britain was ripe for revolution, so landed a 1,400-strong force at Carregwastad Point, on the Pencaer peninsula near Fishguard. The idea was that the men should march to Liverpool, swelling their numbers on their way with disaffected peasants who would be only too happy to overthrow the ruling classes, while a larger force of French arrived by way of Ireland. It was not the first military plan to be compounded more of hope than realism, but this one had a quite rarefied folly about it. The men dumped on the Welsh coast had no clear plan of action, and since they were mostly convicts with no enthusiasm for their mission they spent their brief time before capture looting and getting drunk. The sturdy yeomanry had no difficulty rounding them up, helped – so the story goes – by the mistaken belief of the French that the red flannel cloaks of the local women who lined up to watch the invaders from afar were in fact the uniforms of troops of the line. One of these ladies, an Amazonian figure called Jemima Nicholas, took a more active role in the proceedings by venturing out with a pitchfork and rounding up twelve Frenchmen in a

field. Her memorial is to be found at St Mary's
church in Fishguard, and in the town square the
Royal Oak has an inscription saying that this was
where the terms of the surrender were signed.

The episode, farcical though it was, can be seen
now as offering a hint that the revolutionary ideas
that were to shape the modern world could intrude
even on peaceful Pembrokeshire. There were other
signs too, including the construction of a naval
dockyard at Milford Haven, a town designed to a
gridiron pattern. The stage was set for a period of
rapid changes; with the nineteenth century came a
sequence of events which were to lead, inexorably,
to the Pembrokeshire we know today.

4 Seeking out the busy past

If you stand by the river in the village of Hook, you might think that the place had always been wrapped in rural tranquillity. The Western Cleddau's lucid waters lap creeks where boats ride easily; the curlew's plaintive cry seems the very essence of solitude.

Not so long ago, though, this was a busy mining village where barges tied up at the quay to load the anthracite coal for which Pembrokeshire was famous. At one time there were over a dozen collieries in the area; the last didn't close until 1948.

The remains of tramways and mines are still visible, but the dust, the clamour and the danger have long passed into limbo. The Daugleddau no longer stands for coal, but for a region of the national park which is at once distinctive, restful and surprisingly underrated. It is a place where two rivers meet and wooded hills stand above tidal creeks and mudflats, and whatever the season it is alive with interest for the nature lover.

There are many such viewpoints in the Daugleddau, where the river scenery has a beguiling charm. This inland section of the National Park is often bypassed by tourists making for the coast.

There are villages not far from Hook which share its industrial legacy. Across the water is the quaintly named Landshipping, on the Eastern Cleddau. The first steam engine in the Pembrokeshire coalfield was installed here in 1800 at a cost of £1,900, but nearly half a century later came a disaster which killed forty men and boys and made mining such a dirty word in the community that it ceased entirely shortly afterwards. There were collieries at Reynalton, Yerbeston and Loveston, now peaceful hamlets on the by-roads between the Cleddau Rivers and Saundersfoot, and the shipping points on the Daugleddau included Cresswell Quay, Lawrenny Quay and Llangwm Pool.

The coalfield, which runs in a narrow strip from Carmarthen Bay in the east to St Bride's Bay in the west, was being exploited in Tudor times and by the 1860s it was raising nearly 150,000 tons of coal every year. Some of it came from Saundersfoot, which had

Winter, too, has its prizes for those venturesome enough to visit the National Park off-season. The flesh tingles at the very sight of the frozen Eastern Cleddau at Blackpool Mill, a renovated eighteenth century corn mill just off the A40, six miles east of Haverfordwest.

several quite prosperous collieries in Victorian times. It is to coal that we owe the construction of the harbour at Saundersfoot, now so obviously a haven for the fun-loving that one might imagine no-one had ever dirtied their hands there. There was a railway linking the harbour with local collieries; it ran nearly five miles to Thomas Chapel and had the odd gauge of 4 ft 0$\frac{3}{8}$ in. At first it was worked by horses, but steam was introduced later.

The existence of the railway and harbour led to the growth of other industries in the area. It is on record that at Wiseman's Bridge in 1850 'a colony of people was engaged in turning out the best fire bricks the country could produce', and the Stepaside Ironworks were opened in 1849. A branch of the Saundersfoot Railway ran there, and the nearby Grove Colliery provided coal for the works. A canal and a network of tramways were also part of a busy little industrial complex which, however, had a life-span of only thirty years or so, the competition from less remote areas and a slump in the price of pig iron proving its downfall. Production ceased in 1877, but the workshops were retained for use by neighbouring collieries until 1930. Some of the Ironworks' buildings still stand, much more picturesque in their ruin than they were in their heyday.

The western extremity of the coalfield was at Newgale and Nolton, on St Brides Bay, where sailing ships were loaded with anthracite. Iron rings and mooring stanchions can be seen from the coastal footpath. Look out too for the relics of Trefrân Cliff Colliery, three-quarters of a mile north of Nolton Haven. A forlorn-looking chimney stack still stands, devoid of smoke or usefulness, and an old weighbridge straddles the footpath. Tramways took the coal down to Nolton Haven, where the Folkestone Colliery Company was established in 1769 by Abel Hicks, proud owner of such coastal vessels as the *Industrious Bee*. Nothing is left of the pier he knew, but the little port's Counting House – now a private house – still overlooks the beach.

By today's standards, much of the mining in Pembrokeshire in the nineteenth century was incredibly primitive. In 1853, an inspector of mines reported that methods had changed little since Tudor times, with shallow shafts, insecure tackle and ventilation so bad that the workers had only half the air they required. The miners around Begelly lived in 'clom' cottages made of mud and stones, with no ceiling beneath the thatch. When abandoned, these hovels soon crumbled away to

The mild air of Tenby encourages the growth of plants which are normally seen only in much warmer climes. The town became a fashionable resort in Georgian times, and retains its popularity because it has learned to adapt while preserving its essential character.

nothing. Yet the pay, low though it was, compared well with that of the agricultural labourer, and the miners generally had smallholdings, which made their lot more bearable. Thanks to coal, the growth of Saundersfoot was remarkable. In 1810 it was an obscure hamlet with only six cottages, but by 1856 it was presenting an 'air of bustle and trade' when compared with 'idle Tenby'. Even then, however, it was gradually finding favour with those who had time and wealth enough to go on holiday, and in the 1870s it was reported that the town was attracting visitors from as far afield as London, Birmingham and Oxford. Meanwhile, 'idle Tenby' had established itself as a fashionable resort, with an assembly room where in Georgian times the 'quality' had gathered before entering the Bath House to dip tentative toes in the brine. No doubt they thoroughly approved the inscription put there in 1805 by the architect SP Cockerell: 'The sea washes away all the ills of mankind.' It was, of course, in Greek, to put it clearly out of reach of the lower orders.

In the elitist pleasures of the moneyed classes in Georgian Tenby we can trace the beginnings of modern tourism, yet the notion that a whole industry could develop out of the desire for a break in routine would have struck our forebears as extraordinary. For most people, even a journey outside their own parish was something of an event. Clocks in Pembrokeshire quite accurately told a different time from those in London, as Greenwich Mean Time was not generally adopted in Britain until the spread of railways later in the century. In the Gwaun valley they had not even caught up with

A sprinkling of snow comes even to Tenby when winter turns harsh, and momentarily it transfigures the South Beach, before melting to leave the sands as uniformly tawny as they are in midsummer.

the change to the Julian Calendar, and happily celebrated New Year's Day on the thirteenth of January! The fastest form of transport was the mail coach, driven by a coachman wrapped in layer upon layer of clothing and with a top-hatted guard who peremptorily blew his gleaming 'yard of tin'. The Milford Mail first set out from London in 1785, and by 1830 it was performing the 256-mile journey in thirty-three hours.

The importance of the Milford Mail is that, like the Holyhead Mail through north Wales, it formed a connection with Ireland. Packet boats sailed from Milford Haven to Waterford, and if the coach were late arriving in Milford the Superintendent of Mail Coaches in London wanted to know why. The final hectic stages from Carmarthen were performed by 'unicorn' teams of three horses, and after their exertions the beasts enjoyed the notably slower pace of the return journey, when the coachmen and guard felt relaxed enough to indulge in a spot of rook shooting. On such a hilly route the drag was often in use, and the wheels were sometimes so hot with friction that it was possible to fry bacon on the rims – or so it was claimed at the time!

The stage-coach system was complex and well organized, with a network of inns which not only catered for the traveller but also served as staging posts where one team of horses gave way to another. It provided direct employment for coachmen, guards, booking clerks and the manufacturers and repairers of coaches, and indirect employment for an army of others, not least the chambermaids, waiters and ostlers at the inns which depended so much on this trade. The speed with which it was dismantled might seem, to us, a prime example of the way less sophisticated ages than ours were able to achieve technological revolutions without the slightest regard for social consequences. There were no arguments over alternative jobs or redundancy payments; people were left to cope as best they could. Busy inns degenerated into mere taverns and roads were neglected for over half a century, until the motor car made their good maintenance a matter of national concern again.

It was the mighty Isambard Kingdom Brunel who took Pembrokeshire into the Railway Age. His broad-gauge line reached Haverfordwest in 1854, when the importance of the Irish connection was such that the mayor of Waterford attended the opening ceremony. As the terminus of the line Brunel chose Neyland rather than Milford Haven, adding insult to injury by renaming Neyland 'New Milford'. He had visions of its becoming a transatlantic port, but nothing came of these hopes and in time even the Irish Mails went to Fishguard.

Although Milford Haven was brought on to the South Wales Railway (then being merged with the Great Western Railway) by 1863, its off-hand treatment by Brunel typified its changing fortunes. There had been high hopes for its future late in the eighteenth century, when it was founded on land owned by Sir William Hamilton, best known as the complaisant husband who provided Horatio Nelson with a mistress. It was then attracting settlers from Nantucket Island who, unsettled by the American War of Independence, saw it as a base from which to pursue their calling as whalers. These Quaker families were out to corner the market in sperm oil, a fuel which fed what street lights existed in London, but the invention of coal gas put paid to that idea and they settled for more prosaic trades in the town. Meanwhile, a far greater enterprise was under way. This was the naval dockyard which Charles Greville, Sir William's nephew, had persuaded the Admiralty to establish at Milford. It was Greville who, acting as agent, had possessed the drive and imagination to turn his uncle's vague plans for a new town into reality, and when Nelson himself

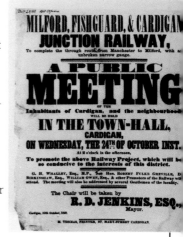

The Manchester to Milford railway project was doomed to failure, but it excited high hopes before dissillusion set in. The reference to 'narrow gauge' is deceptive – it was narrow only in relation to the seven-foot broad gauge which Isambard Kingdom Brunel was busily promoting at the time.

descended on Milford in 1802, the speeches at the banquet in his honour spoke of the citizens' boundless faith in their town's future. Unhappily, a dispute over land persuaded the Admiralty to abandon the dockyard in 1814, and Milford set upon the dispiriting task of finding a new role for itself.

The town's loss, however, was Pembroke's gain, for the Admiralty hit upon the simple expedient of transferring the dockyard across the water. The *Lion*, then the largest warship in the Royal Navy, was launched at Pembroke Dock in 1847, and the largest three-decker ship in the world, the *Duke of Wellington*, followed in 1852. As the century progressed revolutionary changes in shipbuilding occurred, and Pembroke Dock was in the vanguard of the advance. The sailors still had hearts of oak, but they now put to sea in ships of iron. Sail gave way to steam, and Pembroke Dock provided many of the gunboats, destroyers and light cruisers the Navy required.

Such activity encouraged the government to look to the defences of the Haven, and the wonder is that they took so long to do so. As far back as 1539 Thomas Cromwell had emphasized the need for fortifications, and after the Spanish Armada scare of 1588 the Deputy Lieutenant of Pembrokeshire had recommended the siting of forts on Thorn Island, Dale Point and Stack Rock. Nearly three centuries were to pass before much was done, however, and by then the threat was not from Spain, but from France. The Defensible Barracks, designed to hold a garrison of 500 men, were built at Pembroke Dock between 1844 and 1857, with martello towers at either end of the waterfront. A new fort was built at Dale to command the entrance to the Haven, and others at Popton Point, Chapel Bay, South Hook Point and Hubberston, as well as on Thorn Island and Stack Rock. These have come to be known as 'Palmerston's Follies', although they seemed pretty sensible at the time. When Britons lived in fear of invasion from France they could accommodate a total of 1,900 men, who had 220 heavy guns at their command.

If the forts strike us now as mere curiosities, there are other historical episodes which seem even more bizarre. The Manchester and Milford Railway project was intended to provide a link between south-west Wales and the manufacturing towns of Lancashire at a time when it was seriously held that Milford Haven might become a second Liverpool. Milford, however, failed to win the Atlantic trade, and the only part of the Manchester and Milford to be constructed was a forty-two mile stretch of line between Pencader and Aberystwyth. It was the work of that redoubtable entrepeneur David Davies of Llandinam, who also took a railway from Pembroke Dock to Tenby in the face of gloomy predictions that it would fail because of geological difficulties. 'I knew we had hills in the way,' he breezily remarked in an after-dinner speech, 'and that if we could not get over them, we must get under them.' The line was opened in 1863, and later extended through Narberth to join the main London line at Whitland.

As the railways brought visitors to Pembrokeshire in ever increasing numbers, the days when the stage coaches trundled through the countryside began to seem increasingly remote. So, too, was the social unrest which had exploded into the violence of the Rebecca Riots between 1839 and 1844, when tollgates were destroyed by people who thought there were far too many of them. The farmers were especially resentful of this extortion, after a succession of bad harvests. The fervour that led to the smashing and burning of tollgate after tollgate was compounded of a heady brew of revulsion and religion, as the rioters found inspiration in an obscure Biblical text: 'And they blessed Rebekah, and said to her, may your descendants possess the gates of those who hate them.' With a sublime sense of logic which less poetic nations than the Welsh might have thought absurd, they not only adopted the name of Rebecca but actually dressed up as women as they went into battle. The riots began in the Preseli foothills and ended only after a Parliamentary commission had acknowledged the justice of their case.

Religious enthusiasm was, by now, finding more conventional expression in attendance at chapel on a Sunday, and often on several weekdays as well. The Welsh found Nonconformity peculiarly to their taste, partly because the indolence and social pretensions of the eighteenth-century clergy had made a rift between the Established Church and the people. Since independence was implicit in Nonconformity, congregations took delight in vying with one another to obtain the best preachers and the most imposing buildings, and although the chapel is now a spent force socially, the places of worship remain to remind us of this past era. They are of interest architecturally, as a number of influences can be seen at work. Nolton

Congregational (1858) in Nolton Haven and
Wesleyan Methodist (1865) in Haverfordwest are in
the classical style, and so is Rhydwilym Baptist
(1875). Tabernacle Congregational in
Haverfordwest was built in 1874 in the Roman
basilica style, and in the same town Bethesda Baptist,
raised in 1878 at a cost of £2,199, is an example of the
work of the ubiquitous George Morgan of
Carmarthen.

In all chapels, the pulpit has a position of prime
importance, as the sermon is a central feature of the
service. In his cogent and well-illustrated booklet,
'Welsh Chapels', Anthony Jones reminds us that:

> 'The pulpit was appropriately elevated, not only
> to allow the congregation to see the preacher, but
> also to allow him to fix the members with his eagle
> eye and drive home the message to each and
> every person who sat before him. The sermons
> were not abstract disquisitions, but forcefully
> eloquent discourses which would be readily
> understood by the hearers, while the legendary
> power and *hwyl* of the great preachers could
> sway congregations into convulsive ecstasy. The
> pulpit was nearly always the most elaborate
> interior feature of the chapel from which the
> preacher commanded like a captain on the
> bridge of a ship. At Rehobeth, Hakin, Milford
> Haven, the pulpit was so high that some preachers
> refused to ascend to that "perilous perch",
> choosing rather to exhort from the Big Seat.'

When the preachers were at their most fervent, so
was the Welsh Sunday at its strongest as an
institution. At the time there was a lot to be said for it
socially, as it provided a day of much-needed rest
for a hard-working people. Many of the deacons
who sat solemnly on the Sêt Fawr (Big Seat) on a
Sunday could be seen on Monday morning in the
quarries which were an inescapable feature of
nineteenth-century Pembrokeshire. In 1850, roofing
slates were being shipped from Haverfordwest to
many parts of England, and later in the century
shiploads of Pembrokeshire slate were exported
from the 'blue lagoon' quarry at Abereiddy and
from The Parrog at Newport. The most celebrated
order, however, went to the Gilfach quarry at
Llangolman, on the southern slopes of Mynydd
Preseli: it was asked to supply some of the slates for
the Palace of Westminster. In his area guide to the
Preseli Hills, published by the National Park, Brian

There were dreams, once, of turning the secluded village of Rosebush, in the Preseli foothills, into a holiday resort. These came to nothing, but the place today has a quiet charm which entrances visitors.

John explains how these slates were created by the intrusion of igneous rocks into local shales, subjecting them to heat and pressure:

'Close to the edge of a mass of intrusive rock the shales are baked hard; further away they may be altered only slightly, giving rise to slates of rather poorer quality. The Preseli slates vary greatly in their cleavage characteristics, and their colour ranges from purple, red and pink to blue, green and grey. . . . Rosebush slates were dark blue; Temple Druid (Maenclochog) slates were olive-green; Glogue slates were black; and the slate from Foel Drych was largely silver-grey.'

Dr John reminds us that slate was used, at one time, not only for roofing material, but for hearth stones, window sills, pig troughs and even coffins. It was taken long distances by horse and cart, and slate products went by barge from Blackpool Mill on the Eastern Cleddau. The advent of the railways gave a boost to the industry generally, and led to the establishment of an entirely new quarry complex at Rosebush in north Pembrokeshire. The quarries there had a brief but busy life and their success hinged on the service provided by the North Pembroke and Fishguard Railway, which started life as the Narberth Road and Maenclochog Railway.

These cottages at Rosebush once housed the men who worked the nearby quarries, and their families. These quarries, like others in the Preseli Hills, reached their heyday in the second half of the nineteenth century, and the slates went by rail as far as London.

This was built from Clynderwen to Rosebush between 1872 and 1876 to take slates from the Rosebush quarries, which were owned by Sir Hugh Owen, a man of diverse enthusiasms who believed he could make a holiday resort out of this settlement in the Preseli foothills. Artificial lakes were stocked with fish, rhododendrons planted, and the creation of lily ponds gave the final sumptuous touches to this improbable dream. The Precelly Hotel was built to take the rush of tourists who, however, turned out to exist only in the lively imagination of Sir Hugh. In Edwardian times the quarries closed, and although the Great Western Railway, which took over the line, made a brave attempt between the wars to succeed where Sir Hugh had failed, only a few dozen passengers a week were persuaded to make the journey. Today Rosebush still has its charm, as a faded dream often has. It stands off the B4313 between Maenclochog and New Inn, an unsurfaced road leading to the derelict quarries, where the waste tips are clothed with heather and a deep, silent pool reflects the ever-changing skies. In summer there are bilberries to be picked nearby, and in winter icicles hang from the steep slopes above the frozen water. The old cottages where the

The hoppers at Porthgain harbour are among the more unusual relics of Pembrokeshire's industrial past. Stone quarried on the far side of the headland was crushed here before being shipped to many parts of Wales and England.

quarrymen used to live now make a cheerful sight, as instead of being a uniform grey they are picked out in different colours, while the green corrugated-iron hotel is a curiosity, with posters inside dating from the time of those high but misplaced hopes.

Almost due west of Rosebush, on the coast between St David's and Fishguard, is another picturesque relic of Pembrokeshire's industrial past: the coppery-coloured buildings, known as hoppers, at Porthgain harbour where crushed stone was stored before being shipped to many parts of England. They have a foreign, rather Moorish look about them, and are protected by a preservation order. The stone was quarried at Abereiddy, the other side of the headland of Ynys Barry, and sent to Porthgain along a tramroad which also served other quarries. The route of the tramroad can still be seen, and Porthgain itself is a scheduled ancient monument. Abereiddy granite went towards the making of public buildings in London, Liverpool and Dublin and granite chips were used for macadamizing roads. There was also a thriving trade in slate at one time. The quarries were at their busiest at the turn of the century, but went into rapid decline after the First World War. Operations ceased entirely in 1931.

Metal-working has also played a significant role in Pembrokeshire life, and there are traces of copper ore workings on the southern side of the St David's peninsula dating from pre-Roman times. More recently there was a silver-lead mine at

Llanfyrnach, which reached peak production in the 1880s. Coming south we find Blackpool Mill, which stands on the Eastern Cleddau near the point where the A4075 joins the A40 at Canaston Bridge. Its situation alone makes it a tourist attraction, as the woods above the river have a serene beauty at any time of year. Added to this, however, is its historic appeal. There was a busy forge here in the eighteenth century, which gave way to the present mill in 1813. In sailing days schooners laden with grain tied up at the mill, which was in use until 1945. It has now been renovated and, like the French mill at Carew, is open to the public.

One distinctive feature of Pembrokeshire which often escapes the eye of the casual visitor is the number of fine cast-iron railings outside many town houses. There are fine examples in Tenby and Milford Haven, Haverfordwest and Narberth, Fishguard and Newport. Some were brought in by sea, the most notable import being the art nouveau railings in front of the Old Printing House in Solva, but the majority were cast in the county itself. The Woodside Foundry near Tenby specialized in work of this kind, and there were numerous forges and foundries.

The woollen mills were also a useful source of employment. There were thirty of these in Pembrokeshire at the turn of the century, and although the craft of weaving is still flourishing only two of the old mills remain: one at Wallis, near Woodstock, ten miles north-east of Haverfordwest just off the B4329 and the other at Tregwynt, near St Nicholas, about three miles north of Mathry.

As the Victorian era gave way to the brief Edwardian flourish before the onslaught of war, the sea continued to play a dominant role in Pembrokeshire's destiny. The discovery of rich fishing grounds west of the British Isles had a dramatic impact on the county in general and the town of Milford Haven in particular: at last it found a new role, after the disappointments of the nineteenth century. It became the home of a rapidly expanding trawler fleet which made it the sixth largest fishing port in Britain. In the years leading up to the First World War there were over sixty trawlers in Milford, and the industry employed about 2,000 local people. This success compensated for the town's failure to become a second Liverpool by capturing the transatlantic trade, an ambition which did not seem to be as hopelessly ambitious in the 1880s as it does today. Instead of another

Liverpool, Milford became a Welsh Grimsby, and remained so until the years following the Second World War, when the trade went into steady and irreversible decline. The best year was 1946, when more than 59,000 tons of fish were landed.

Meanwhile, Pembroke Dock had undergone a cruel reversal of fortune. Its dockyard had worked at full stretch in the First World War, but this counted for nothing when the Admiralty coldly assessed the cost of its remoteness in the hard economic climate of the 1920s, and the closure of the dockyard in 1926 seemed at the time pitiless and unforgivable. It took another war to bring new life to the dockyard; part of it was used as a naval base for ship-repairing. Pembroke Dock was also the nerve-centre for mine-laying operations and a major convoy base in the Second World War, and its oil storage tanks invited the attention of the Luftwaffe, which raided the town many times.

It is well to note, here, the part played in peace and war by the lighthouses of Pembrokeshire. The one at St Ann's Head has a history which can be taken back as far as the Middle Ages, when warning lights for ships were being placed on this dangerous headland. This is, in fact, one of the oldest lighthouses along the whole of the western seaboard, and there was a time when it was the only light between the Scillies and the Isle of Man. There are other lights on the Smalls, South Bishop, Strumble Head, Caldey and Skokholm. The one at Caldey has the distinction of being the oldest lighthouse *building* in Pembrokeshire, dating from around 1810; the Skokholm lighthouse, established in 1916, is the youngest.

Away from the western seaboard, fishing craft have plied the quiet waters of the Daugleddau from time immemorial. At one time the villagers of Llangwm – which is invariably pronounced 'Langham' by the locals – lived entirely by fishing, and there was even a distinctive Llangwm boat, rather like an updated coracle. At one time cockles, oysters and mussels were gathered at low tide, but the trade has died out now. At Llangwm and nearby Hook, however, fishermen still catch salmon by means of a technique known as compass netting, so called because the net is fixed between two poles which resemble the points of a compass. This mode of fishing has been part of Pembrokeshire life for so long that one might be deceived into thinking it originated there, but in fact it was introduced from Gloucestershire around 1800.

Sheep farming is an important economic activity in Pembrokeshire, and the Preseli Hills are speckled with flocks hardy enough to survive even the harshest winter.

Llangwm once had a reputation for taking insularity to the point of violence, and the women were apparently more aggressive than the men, stoning strangers on sight. Another dubious claim to fame was the absence of a village pub, due to the fact that the local landowner was a total abstainer. There is now no difficulty in quenching one's thirst in Llangwm, and the female of the species is neither more nor less fearful than anywhere else.

Above all, Pembrokeshire is an agricultural county. It is famous for its early potatoes, and the fertile soils, long growing period and relatively frost-free climate of its coastal regions encourage the highly specialized production of these. Inland, dairy farming is dominant in low-lying areas, while the thinner soils of the Preseli Hills favour sheep farming and beef production. Farms are generally small to medium in size, the vast majority of them being under one hundred acres in extent. The larger farms tend to be on the Dale and Angle peninsulas, where the existence of big estates has reflected the social pattern of the Norman occupation. The Angle peninsula contains the largest farm in the whole of the national park, exceeding 1,000 acres. A big change took place between 1964 and 1973, when the number of smallholdings in the park was halved by the amalgamation of units.

Another change in farming pattern concerns the type of crops we find. Cereal growing, particularly of winter-sown varieties, has become more popular in coastal areas. The acreage of improved grassland has increased, too, with a corresponding decrease in that of early potatoes and rough grazing.

The decisions a farmer makes clearly have a direct effect on the landscape. When a hedge is removed, the whole ecology alters. Changes of this kind have been small, especially in comparison with other parts of Britain. Removing hedges is a costly business, and they are useful not only as boundaries but as protection for livestock and crops in this windswept region.

These field margins and boundaries are of intense interest to the naturalist. In contrast, ploughed fields and areas of improved grassland have low wildlife value. Odd corners unsuitable for ploughing, however, are sometimes left rough and provide homes for a variety of plant and animal life, especially if they contain ponds.

The biggest change affecting this national park since its inception has undoubtedly been the development of Milford Haven as an oil port. The first signs of this came in the 1950s, when both BP and Esso announced plans to bring crude oil to the UK in vessels up to 100,000 tons. In 1958 the newly created Milford Haven Conservancy Board was given the task of protecting and improving the deepwater facilities in the Haven, and seven years later the first 100,000-ton vessel, the *British Admiral*, berthed on her maiden voyage. Between 1967 and 1970 the largest rock-dredging operation ever attempted in any port in the world was carried out, with the aim of straightening out and widening the existing channel rather than deepening it. As a result, vessels up to 275,000 deadweight tons were able to enter and berth on any tide, and sometimes it was possible to accommodate even larger vessels. The improvements included the placing of 'leading lights' at the mouth of the Haven, to bring the biggest ships safely through the 1,300-foot entrance channel. In 1969, the first 250,000-tonner ever to enter a British port, the Esso *Scotia*, arrived on her maiden voyage and for a while four or more vessels categorized as super-super-tankers – very large crude carriers or 'VLCCs' – arrived weekly.

By 1974 there were five oil terminals and four refineries on the shores of the Haven, plus a major oil-fired power station, and more than £330 million had been spent on the development of industry directly dependent on the port. In that year Milford Haven became Britain's largest port in terms of shipping tonnage and cargo handled. It is still the biggest oil port in the country, but the recession and the discovery of North Sea oil have combined to bring about a considerable reduction in the port's traffic. This has been reflected in the scaling down of operations by the companies which went there when prospects were brightest. At one time BP had a sixty-two-mile pipeline taking crude oil from its deepwater terminal on the south shore of the Haven to its refinery at Llandarcy, but operations ceased in 1985. By then the Esso refinery, which had been the first to be built and at one time accounted for about a quarter of Milford Haven's oil traffic, was no more, a serious blow to the port's prosperity. In the meantime, Texaco and Gulf had joined forces to build a catalytic cracker complex, enabling them to produce more light-oil products such as petrol, and Amoco had developed a similar plant in conjunction with Murco Ltd.

While the future of the oil industry in Pembrokeshire, and the extent to which the search for off-shore gas might be pursued, remained problematical in the mid-1980s, tourism continued to expand. By then the number of visitors to the region was put at 1.2 million a year, most of them arriving by car from South-East England and the West Midlands. 'Idle Tenby' was not so idle now, and the National Park Authority had the task of providing the framework in which people might enjoy the beauty of the region, while preserving the tranquillity which is the essence of its popularity.

5 **Nature at the crossroads**

Pembrokeshire is internationally renowned for its plant and animal life. Its colonies of sea birds make it a paradise for ornithologists, and its flowers colour the landscape at all seasons: even in January more than fifty species are in bloom, and at the coming of spring nature runs riot in the country lanes and on the clifftops.

The variety of wildlife in this national park means it has supreme interest both for the casual visitor and for naturalists with expert knowledge. People travel far to see the guillemots cluster on jagged rocks where the Atlantic rollers break at the foot of precipitous cliffs, or to hear the Manx shearwaters come screaming back to the islands on a summer night – a thrilling and unforgettable sound. But there are a host of other pleasures to be gained, all the more intense, very often, for being unsought: the sudden sight of sheets of bluebells and pink campion, the heady scent of gorse, the plaintive cry of curlew. Whether you are merely passing through the park or making a carefully planned visit, this will be an enriching experience.

Ecologically, Pembrokeshire is a kind of crossroads, due to its position on the fringe of the European landmass. It marks the western limit of many terrestrial life forms, while its coastal waters are the eastern limit of many aquatic species. Again, this peninsula, and its off-shore islands, is the most northerly area reached by marine creatures dependent on the warm waters of the Gulf Stream, or North Atlantic Drift, and the most southerly place in which several Arctic species of fish and sea birds are to be found.

The climate, which is similar to that of the Channel Islands and west Cornwall, plays an important part in providing the conditions in which a variety of plant and animal life may flourish. Dale is the sunniest place in Wales, and since the mean minimum temperature on the Pembrokeshire coast is 4°C (40°F) plant growth is dormant for only about 115 days. The rainfall is low along the coast, averaging thirty-five inches a year, but rises to

Pembrokeshire is renowned for its sheer variety of wild flowers. There are hardy plants in bloom even in January, while others await the coming of spring.

The lesser black-backed gull nests on the ground and lays a clutch of two or three eggs at the end of April or in the first weeks of May.

The razorbill, emblem of the Pembrokeshire Coast National Park, nests in colonies, often near the related guillemot. Both species can be seen on Stack Rocks (Elegug Stacks), on the Castlemartin peninsula.

eighty inches in the Preseli Hills. Species of sub-alpine plants have survived in the area covered by the national park since the last stages of the Ice Age, and are to be found nowhere else in Britain. Other plants, characteristic of periods warmer than ours, flourish in sheltered places on the coast, benefiting from the exceptionally mild climate. So, intriguingly, Pembrokeshire has preserved aspects of the past, making it a kind of living museum of botanical oddities. There are also some purely local varieties of common species of plant and animal, such as the Tenby daffodil – of which more later – the Llangwm herring and the Skomer vole.

When we think of the natural history of Pembrokeshire, however, it is the bird life that comes most readily to mind; not for nothing is the emblem of the national park a razorbill. This large black and white bird, a member of the auk family, is to be found in huge numbers along the coast and on the islands. Stack Rocks and the Castlemartin peninsula, shown on the Ordnance Survey map as Elegug Stacks, is probably the best-known auk colony in the British Isles. There are about 130 pairs of razorbills and 1,000 pairs of guillemots on these rocks, as well as fulmars, shags and kittiwakes. The colony is occupied continuously from late April or early May until the end of July and a visit to the site, where that geological curiosity known as The Green Bridge of Wales is another attraction, should be high on anyone's list.

The bird life on the islands is dealt with in a later chapter – suffice to say, here, that in the breeding season there are no fewer than 35,000 pairs of Manx shearwaters on Skokholm and perhaps as many as 100,000 pairs on Skomer. The peculiar habits of this bird, however, mean that most visitors to the park rarely see it: in the breeding season the female is underground all day, incubating its egg, and its mate comes in from its fishing expeditions only at night! There are good reasons for this apparently bizarre behaviour, because in daylight it would be at the mercy of predators such as the greater black-backed gull. The puffin, which can be seen on boat trips to Skomer and Skokholm, is another curiosity. It flies underwater as well as in the air, and in terms of evolution stands somewhere between a penguin and an ordinary bird. One of its more endearing features is the clumsiness of movement: because its wingspan is too small for its body it appears to be ill-adapted for flight, yet manages to fly great distances.

A contrast in light and shade near Rosebush, which lies in the foothills of Mynydd Preseli.

The cormorant is as skilful in catching fish as it is voracious in eating them. It can consume more than its own weight of fish in a day and is a strong underwater swimmer, pressing its wings to its body and propelling itself forward with thrusts of its webbed feet. These large, reptilian-looking birds – black from a distance, though with a green sheen – often fly to inland waters, passing over Haverfordwest on the way to and from the reservoirs at Rosebush and Llys-y-fran. The shag is similar to the cormorant in appearance but smaller, and lacks the cormorant's white face-patch. It also has different habits, rarely entering estuaries but preferring to fish in clearer waters off the coast. The tall and stately heron is most decidedly an estuary bird, and if indiscreet enough to venture to the islands is ruthlessly harried by gulls. There are several heronries in Pembrokeshire, the largest of which is in Slebech Park.

The group of birds known as waders are mostly passage migrants or winter visitors, but one of them, the oystercatcher, is a familiar sight throughout the year. With its handsome plumage and long orange bill it is the most conspicuous of our shore birds, and its piping note is unmistakable. Another wader, the curlew, has a more melancholy cry. Once confined to moorland, it now breeds in all kinds of damp, open country and often feeds in flocks in winter, wading over coastal mudflats and marches.

Ducks are present in the park in great numbers. In winter some rare species may be seen in Pickleridge Pools, The Gann, near Dale, and in nearby Bicton Pool. The more common winter visitors include the widgeon, a highly gregarious bird which frequents the Cleddau estuaries, the River Pembroke and Angle Bay. Flocks of teal also gather on the Cleddau, but the garganey – otherwise known as summer teal – is only seen in small numbers during March and April, favouring the shallow pool on Trefeiddan Moor near St David's. Look out for the red-breasted merganser in early spring: the drake is recognized by the untidy double crest on a head that looks almost black from a distance, but is in fact dark green.

Some bird lovers would say that one of the best reasons for visiting this national park is the chance it provides of observing the chough, which is now a rarity in Britain. Pembrokeshire is in fact a stronghold of this red-billed member of the crow family, which has the peculiarity of being an alpine bird on the Continent and a clifftop bird in Britain. It is acrobatic, like the raven, sometimes diving with wings almost closed tight and then soaring in the updraught at the cliff's edge. The cliffs and caves are also the haunt of the rock dove, which is the ancestor of all our pigeons, both the homing variety and those which strut around our towns and cities in search of scraps. This inoffensive creature is at the mercy of the peregrine falcon, which swoops on its prey at speeds of up to 180 miles an hour. The peregrine has itself been the victim of falconers, and in the reign of James II a record £1,000 was paid for a pair. It was killed off in great numbers in the Second World War in order to protect the humble carrier pigeon, and later suffered from the use of pesticides, which were sprayed on the crops and absorbed into the bodies of its prey. Small wonder that between 1956 and 1962 the number of breeding pairs in the British Isles fell from around 650 to below seventy. These pesticides are now banned and the number of peregrines in the national park has risen to the maximum the area can support.

The most conspicuous bird of prey in Pembrokeshire is undoubtedly the buzzard. The laziness of its flight masks the sharpness of its intention: as it idly sails across farmland or moor, it is scanning the ground below for small mammals and insects. Kestrels also occur along the coast and in such inland areas as the Gwaun valley and the Preseli Hills, and the native trees of sessile oak, ash, sycamore and hazel provide cover for warblers as well as blackcap, chiffchaff and, more rarely, the redstart. By fast-flowing streams look out for the dipper, perching on stones in mid-stream and plunging its head in and out of the water. The grey wagtail, which in defiance of its name has a bright yellow breast, flits along the surface of mountain streams, and if you're lucky you may see a kingfisher streak by like a flash of blue light. On the heights of Mynydd Preseli, meadow pipits and skylarks abound, and wheatears nest amid the cairns. Here too the curlew's cry is heard, and in autumn snow buntings sometimes appear.

The largest mammal in the national park is the seal, which can be seen lazing on the rocks or swimming in the white surf. The species found in Pembrokeshire is the grey or Atlantic seal, and the breeding grounds are among the largest in the British Isles. Seals are such fine natural swimmers that they are able to reach the west of Ireland or Brittany within a few months of birth, and it is not unknown for them to go as far as Spain.

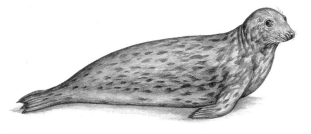

Some of the largest breeding grounds in Britain of the grey or Atlantic seal are to be found around the Pembrokeshire coast. Often only the head of the seal can be seen, bobbing up and down in the surf.

There are whales not far off the coast of Pembrokeshire and from time to time a dead one is washed ashore. Happily, dolphins are seen when they are still alive, and they sometimes come to stay in a particular spot. To the delight of local people and holiday-makers, Solva harbour had its very own dolphin for several months in 1985. Porpoises can also be seen sporting close to shore.

There have never been any deer in the Deer Park – the name was a status symbol only – but since the 1970s there have been red deer on Ramsey Island. There is also a deer farm near Fishguard, from which breeding stock is exported to many overseas countries. The tiny muntjac, also known as the Chinese barking deer, is sometimes sighted in the

Daugleddau, where the thick undergrowth provides ideal cover for a shy creature only two feet tall. It still makes an exotic sight in the Welsh countryside, as it was first introduced to Woburn in the nineteenth century and until quite recently existed only in the grounds of great houses and zoos. The polecat is quite common in Pembrokeshire, though rarely seen. The beaver, which swam the Teifi in medieval times and may have survived until the Tudors, has long since disappeared. Nature is forever changing, and one species gives way to another: the feral mink has broken out of the confines of mink farms and is now well established along rivers and tributaries.

A harmless diversion is to try to identify the various kinds of butterfly. Nearly forty of the seventy-odd species to be found in Britain as a whole occur in Pembrokeshire, including the purple hairstreak, the painted lady and the clouded yellow. Remember that *on no account should a butterfly be killed*; the Victorian trophy hunters who rushed around with butterfly nets would themselves be numbered among the unpleasant species of wildlife today. The camera is a much more life-enhancing device; take a photograph, but leave each habitat as you find it. Chasing a butterfly, even with friendly intent, is a tiring and futile occupation: simply follow its flight, watch where it settles and then approach carefully from behind. If your movements are slow and deliberate, you can come to within a few inches of the creature.

The plant life in Pembrokeshire is rich and varied. The country lanes have distinctive high banks of earth and stone, often crowned by trees bent into strange, stunted shapes by the westerly winds. Here spring comes early, bringing the delicate snowdrop. Primroses, some of the pink variety, come shyly into flower, and then the starry celandines appear. White scurvy grass grows in the lanes and on the clifftops as March gives way to April, and with every week that passes new colours appear on nature's canvas. Sea pinks mingle with the spikes of purple sea milkwort on exposed turf, and the hawthorn blooms in May. Now, too, masses of bluebells give the landscape a new and vivid tone, while the red campion adds variety to the scene. On slopes exposed to the sea spray and full force of the wind, tussocks of thrift show up in a variety of shades from deep crimson to pale pink. Look out for the humble lichens which spread across outcrops on rock in patterns of grey, brown

Clusters of flowers give a brightness to the fields overhanging the river scenery which is an underrated feature of the Pembrokeshire Coast National Park.

Sea pinks dance in the breeze beside the Pembrokeshire Coast Path. Even in January, more than fifty species of flower are in bloom in the National Park.

and vivid orange. It's amazing what sustenance such flowers as the English stone-crop and spurrey can find even in tiny cracks in the rock. Ox-eye daisies spread across the cliffs and small clovers grow on the coast path amid sea storksbill and hart's-horn plantain.

As the spring flowers fade, summer blooms appear. Remember that the more exposed the coast is, especially to salt-laden winds, the greater is its floral diversity. There are no fewer than ten rare sea-cliff species in the park, including the spiked speedwell and the hairy greenweed, and the sea-cliff vegetation of St David's Head and Strumble Head is of particular botanical value.

June and July are the time of dog roses and

honeysuckle, and the hedgebanks are bright with sorrel, rough chervil, hogweed and the yellow cat's ear, which resembles the dandelion. The moorland areas have their beauty too; on the Preseli Hills look out for the flowering heads of hairgrass in the hedgerows, and heather and ling on the heaths. The bilberry is also common, but the steady cropping of this juicy plant by the sheep and ponies that graze the hills means that it is most easily found on hedgebanks and in the less accessible places. In July and August the yellow spikes of bog asphodel appear, while the white cotton sedge gives the marshy areas a haunting beauty. Look out too for the ivy-leaved bellflower, and the pale velvety leaves of St John's wort. The rarer plants include bog myrtle, cranberry, bog orchid, long-leaved sundew and hare's-tail cotton sedge.

The heath and bog vegetation of the St David's peninsula is broadly akin to that of the Preseli Hills, but there are different varieties of local and uncommon plants. Orchids are well represented by five species: the common marsh orchid, dwarf purple orchid, heath spotted orchid, twayblade and lesser butterfly orchid. In May and early June, the pinkish-white flowers of the bogbean bring new beauty to the normally dark waters of the deep pools in old clay pits on Dowrog Moor, and the sombre browns of the dying bracken match the reflective mood of autumn. It is now that the purple heather comes into its own, inviting even the most diffident hikers to stretch their legs for an hour or two.

Parts of the Gwaun valley have been designated as sites of special scientific interest. Several extensive areas have been leased to the National Park Authority and the woodland includes oak, ash, sycamore, alder, blackthorn, hazel, hornbeam, wild cherry and wych elm. This is one of the last remaining haunts of the otter, and the buzzard and raven are also seen.

It's far easier to enjoy the delights of the Gwaun valley with the opening up of the Golden Road Path by the Park Authority. This exhilarating walk takes one from Lower Town, Fishguard, to Crymych via the ridge of the Preseli Hills. It can be viewed as a journey through time, as the path follows the course of the prehistoric trade route taken by those carrying gold from Ireland to the Continent. It makes a fascinating contrast with a walk in the most southerly section of the park. The Carew River Jubilee Walk, opened in 1985 to mark the fiftieth

In May and early June swathes of bluebells and red campion delight the eye on Skomer, an island rich in evidence of ancient occupation. The standing stone is of uncertain origin.

anniversary of the Ramblers' Association, is mainly through deciduous woodland. It provides a glimpse of the shiny, green-leaved shrub known as butchers' broom, once used for scrubbing butchers' slabs. This can be found in the woods near Ford Bridge, and later there is a view of Upton Castle, famous for its stunning collection of exotic trees and shrubs as well as native species. There is always something in flower, and the Indian bean tree is just one of the rarities. The grounds, which include a chapel containing the effigy of a giant of a man who may have been a medieval lord of Upton, are mananged by the Park Authority under an agreement with the owners.

Nine miles to the south-west are the equally famous Bosherston Pools, which now form part of a national nature reserve taking in the cliffs as far as Stackpole Head. The pools were artificially created on limestone, and the non-acidic waters have proved an ideal environment for waterlilies, which are at their best in June. The pools make up the largest expanse of open water in the national park, and are a haven for water-fowl and waders.

The sand dunes provide another distinctive habitat. They contain attractive plants like the sea holly, with its spiny blue-green leaves and blue flower heads, the burnet rose, sea bindweed, blue fleabane, sea pansy and ambiguously named ploughman's spikenard. On the Angle peninsula much of Gupton Burrows has been reclaimed for agriculture but the National Trust and the National Park Authority are opposing any more conversion of this kind, seeing the dunes as of national value for the environment they provide for a wide variety of flowers of sand and heath.

In the Gann estuary, near Dale, cockles are to be found on the mudflats when the tide goes out, and the salt marshes provide a home for a variety of plants. The sea meadow grass comes in June, to be followed in July by the sea aster, the sea purslane with its mealy grey leaves and yellowish fluffy flowers, and the purple sea lavender.

There are more varieties of seaweed than the uninitiated might think – over 800 species are to be found around the coast of Britain. The sea lettuce and bladder wrack are among the most common, but look out too for the whip-like brown fronds of the bootlace weed on the lower shore and the delicate green tufts of sea moss.

Finally, let's turn to a Pembrokeshire speciality – the Tenby daffodil! Unhappily, this distinctive dwarf, which flowers early and is a peculiarly brilliant shade of yellow, has virtually disappeared in the wild, due to the greed of Victorian plunderers who took it away by the thousand. No fewer than half a million bulbs were dispatched to London in a two-year period; little wonder that few remained by the turn of the century. Here and there, the Tenby daffodil can still be found in old cottage gardens, and if you're lucky you may still come across it in village hedgerows in the region of Narberth, Meidrym and Crymych. Tenby Museum is a source of further information for the enthusiast.

The Tenby daffodil is a distinctive dwarf species still to be found in old cottage gardens and some hedgerows. It was plentiful until late in the nineteenth century, when hundreds of thousands of bulbs were uprooted and sent to London.

6 **Those off-shore islands**

There is something especially appealing about islands. If they are small enough they make us think of smugglers' coves, treasure trove, pirate ships flying the skull-and-crossbones and bottles of rum hidden away in the bracken.

The off-shore islands of Pembrokeshire really did harbour pirates at one time, for the Viking raiders of the ninth and tenth centuries surely qualify as such. Superb seamen and fierce warriors, they steered their longboats unerringly through the tidal races, and gave us the names of Skomer and Skokholm, Ramsey and Grassholm, Gateholm and Caldey.

The islands are peaceful today, if one discounts the constant fight for survival that is at the heart of nature. They are places internationally famous as breeding grounds for birds, and where wild

In spring, the cliffs of Skokholm are awash with colour as the bluebells and pinks come into their own. The bays bear romantic names, and it is easy to see why the island has cast a spell over such as the naturalist R M Lockley, who lived here many years.

flowers grow in profusion. Skomer is a national nature reserve, and most of the other islands are also reserves of one kind or another. The first bird observatory in Britain was established on Skokholm in 1933 by the naturalist R M Lockley, who farmed there from 1927 to 1939. Grey seals breed in caves on Ramsey, and Grassholm is one of the very few gannetries in England and Wales.

While writing this book I made two memorable trips to Skokholm and Skomer, in the excellent company of David Matthews, of the Pembrokeshire Coast National Park, and photographer Gareth Davies, of the Five Arches Press in Tenby. The abiding impressions are of myriads of sea birds wheeling and gliding, the blue and pink haze of wild flowers on the headlands, crumbly burrows where shearwaters hide and, most of all, the sense of being at one remove from what we call civilization.

The first trip was to Skokholm on a humid day early in June. We gathered at Martin's Haven, near Marloes, after parking in the National Trust car park on the clifftop. Apart from David and Gareth, there were fifteen or twenty others, some with young children, all with cameras or binoculars. The M290 motor boat of the Dale Sailing Company arrived on time and we clambered aboard, with the cheerful assistance of the two-man crew, and soon we were chugging across Jack Sound and past Tusker Rock. David, whose black beard gave him a piratical look happily belied by his engaging personality, kept up a running commentary as we steadily ploughed the sea to Skokholm. 'That's Midland Island to the right. You'll find kittiwakes there, as well as guillemots and razorbills. . . . Bench Rock to the left – so low it doesn't even show up on radar. . . .' A cormorant dried itself out on a stump of rock just ahead. 'It's got no oil gland to waterproof its feathers – if it didn't dry out it would sink next time it went fishing!'

The first puffins caused as much commotion in the boat as they made in the air with their frenzied, whirring wing-beats; is it simply their comparative rarity that makes them so appealing, or does their slightly comical appearance have something to do with it as well? That brightly coloured bill is made for lampooning, but has a practical use as a weapon and tool for digging. The puffin is, in fact, a pretty practical bird, with a no-nonsense attitude to its young. After feeding its chicks on a rich diet of sand eels for five weeks it then deserts them, leaving them to make their own way to the shore; they learn to fly – if they're lucky – by falling off a cliff, but every year there's a substantial casualty list of puffins which either drown or fall victim to the greater black-backed gull.

As we drew nearer to the island there were birds everywhere – kittiwakes soaring, gulls circling, guillemots strung out along the water like ships of the line. 'They dive to avoid traffic!' said David with a smile as the guillemots plunged out of sight at our approach.

By now the few white buildings on top of the island were clearly visible, and the bands of Old Red Sandstone in the cliff face stood out as emphatically as if purpose-made for a geology lesson.

Equally emphatic was the lady who pushed herself out from a position high on the cliff above us as we drew close to the quay. Dressed in the style of the 1850s, and a little wooden in her manner – in fact entirely wooden in her construction – she turned out to be Alice Williams, figurehead of the schooner of that name, wrecked in 1927. She was put there by the redoubtable Lockley, who in his splendid book *Dream Island Days* – a record of his life on Skokholm – tells us how he bought the entire wreck for £5, 'anchors and chains not included'.

Another party of visitors to Skokholm arrives from Martin's Haven. After scrambling out of the launch they face a steady climb to the bird observatory, which has provided vital information on various species.

We scrambled out of the boat – there's no sedate walk along a gangplank on trips to Skokholm and Skomer – and were met by a flaxen-haired young man who introduced himself as Rob, the warden. Behind him we trailed up a path fringed with clouds of white campion, until we reached those white buildings, which are in fact the bird observatory and warden's living quarters. Here we had some statistics on shearwaters – there are 35,000 pairs of them on Skokholm, quoth Rob – and a word of warning. He reminded us that the shearwater squats in a burrow all day long, to be joined at night by its mate.

'There are sometimes only a couple of inches between your foot and where the bird is incubating its egg,' he reminded us. 'It's easy for your foot to go right into the burrow – in fact a woman's shoe did exactly that the other day!' We all looked disapproving, and wondered how she'd got out of the place alive.

'Please stay right on the footpath,' he pleaded. 'It's either obvious, or marked by white stones. It means you have to go single file in places.'

We trooped into a tiny shop selling postcards, books and guides of various kinds. I bought a pamphlet on *Flora of Skokholm* and, more interestingly, a map of the island which seemed straight from the pages of a children's adventure

The warden on Skokholm has a variety of tasks, not least that of welcoming visitors and telling them what can be found on the island. A note of warning is occasionally sounded; it's easy to harm such a finely-balanced ecology.

story, with Spy Rock, Hog Bay, Orchid Bog and The Devil's Teeth. Who needs the Famous Five?

Outside again, Rob confided that some people asked him if he didn't miss television: 'I say no, I'd rather watch the puffins than *Dallas*!' He's on the island from May to October and finds plenty to do, looking after boat people like ourselves, making counts of birds, carrying out maintenance work and taking courses for enthusiasts. There is also, inevitably, the paperwork.

We set off on a tour of the island and stopped by an old lime kiln, shaped roughly like a huge egg cup stuck in the ground. Its stone walls were covered inside by flowers and other vegetation. As we peered solemnly into it, a blackbird suddenly flew out from its cover. 'I expect he'll get over this shock,' said Rob with a grin. But would we?

Mr Blackbird has company; storm petrels also nest in holes in the kiln. Around it were masses of bluebells; they feel at home in the bracken, which provides them with a similar habitat to a woodland. The sea pink is there in abundance too. And just below the clifftop, there are bright yellow patches of kidney vetch.

We walked on, past Peter's Bay to North Haven. A buzzard flew around the headland, perching half-way down the cliff. The beauty of these Pembrokeshire cliffs is astounding: here the grit band was a delicate pink, and lines of quartz seemed the purest artistry.

Over Northern Plain we went – it sounds like a route march, but was only a matter of a few hundred yards – and there, on open ground, were two spotted eggs of the lesser black-backed gull.

This green, open landscape bears few signs of human habitation; even the drystone walls on Skokholm blend so perfectly with the grass and heather that they seem like natural growths.

Suddenly warfare broke out: two gulls fought on the ground a dozen yards away, wings flapping, beaks pecking at each other's throats. Nature red in tooth and claw. . . .

We passed a drystone wall where storm petrels nest in holes. Rob pointed out a nesting box slotted neatly into the wall. The work of some kind-hearted philanthropist, perhaps? Not quite; scientific curiosity was at the heart of it. 'A man doing research into the storm petrel for his PhD put it there some time ago,' explained Rob. 'He weighed the eggs and the chicks and so on.' And what else? 'Well, all sorts of things. He carried out observations over a long period. One of the things he found out was that the mother didn't come in to feed the chicks if the wind was stronger than Force 7.'

Wise old mother; self-preservation before maternalism. We pondered it as we made for Twinlet Bay. Islands like this are a good place for pondering; the absence of cars, trannies, telly and the press of humanity in general is a wonderful aid to reflection. So, too, are the small reminders of mortality one finds strewn across the grass. Tiny bones of birds, feathers, empty shells; one or two of the children began collecting them. What would become of all these little relics back home in Surbiton?

On again, past Purple Bay and Mad Bay to Tabernacle Rock! How far to Treasure Island? Rob tells us that no snow has ever been recorded on Skokholm, and that frosts are very rare. David points out a rabbit, so still and so brown that it blends perfectly with the tussocky vegetation. The Normans used the island as a warren; Skokholm and Skomer rabbits helped to feed the garrison at Pembroke Castle. More recently black rabbits and chinchilla have been introduced, as well as brown and white – known as Dutch – rabbits. I asked about myxomatosis, and was told it had never reached Skokholm because the island's rabbits had no fleas!

The lighthouse on Skokholm is very white, very neat and wholly automatic; when it was manned it had three keepers – in fact there are three keepers to every manned lighthouse, and David tells us why. It's a grisly tale of the Smalls lighthouse, far out beyond Grassholm, around 1800. 'There were only two men on duty there in those days, and one of them died. The other man was terrified of being accused of murdering him, as they'd quarrelled openly in a pub before going back on duty in the lighthouse. So instead of pushing the corpse into the

The trim white lighthouse on Skokholm serves to remind us that the seas off Pembrokeshire have taken a cruel toll of human life. Automation has removed the need for long, lonely vigils by lighthousemen, who had to be a special breed to endure such isolation.

sea, he made a rough coffin and strapped it to the lantern rail. He tried to attract the attention of passing ships, but since the light was still working and apparently everything was all right none of them took any notice. It was three months before relief came, and by then he was demented. So after that it became the rule to have three keepers to a lighthouse.'

Soberly digesting this tale, we slowly made our way back to the warden's house. By now I'd developed a thirst, and happily accepted Rob's invitation to sample the local brew. This consisted of water bright, which is now hydraulically pumped from the well; it tasted almost as good as a foamy pint of best. The ship's wheel from the Alice Williams hangs in the kitchen; Lockley put it there, and called this building The Wheelhouse.

And now it was time to stroll down to the quay again, reinforced by a final tale of a horse called Sugar Back, which used to pull cartloads of provisions up to the lighthouse along a tramway. 'They called him that,' explained Rob, 'because if you gave him some sugar he gave it back to you.' Don't ask why; folk memory stretches only so far.

A week later David, Gareth and I were back at Martin's Haven again, our party reinforced this time by the addition of my wife, Dorothy. Our destination

The Skomer coastline has an unsurpassed beauty, and the cliffs overlooking the Atlantic rollers have a tale to tell. The outcrops of whitish rock were once lava flows, for – strange as it seems now – this was once a region of active volcanoes.

this time was Skomer, which is three times bigger than Skokholm – 722 acres against 240 acres – and closer to shore, a mere ten minutes away in the *Dale Princess*. The wardens here are Stephen and Anna Sutcliffe; Stephen was a business manager before becoming an islander. Like Rob on Skokholm, he was cheerfully informative but offered a friendly warning or two. 'Remember that there's a light, sandy soil on the clifftop. If you wander off the path you may end up at the bottom of the cliff instead of the top, which isn't healthy.'

There are even more shearwaters here than on Skokholm; 100,000 pairs of them. If you're lucky you may see a chough – 'it's a rare bird but there are two pairs breeding on Skomer' – and the short-eared owl is also present. 'They take a half-hour rest, bomb around for food for their young and then rest again.'

Apart from being larger than Skokholm, Skomer has far more visitors – no fewer than 7,000 of them, between Easter and October. The Neck, the promontory jutting out east of the warden's house, was forbidden territory when I made my visit – 'it's got lots of gull roosts,' explained David, 'and there's a limit to the extent that visitors can be allowed to wander around because of the disturbance to the environment.'

It was a much brighter day than before, and on the mainland Mynydd Preseli was clearly visible. So were the chimney stacks of the refineries at Milford, but at that distance I didn't think they took anything away from the view. A future age might even consider them as interesting and mysterious as we regard the cromlechs. ('What were they for? Many theories have been advanced. . . .') Skomer encourages speculations like this, as it has signs of ancient occupation. If you're at all interested in old settlements, be sure to buy the archaeological guide to the prehistoric farmers of Skomer, as well as the more general guide, both of which are modestly priced and available on the island.

One of the first sights one comes across is the standing stone overlooking North Haven known as the Harold Stone, 'an uninscribed and unshaped monolith of unknown origin', in the words of the guide. Then there are the boundaries of ancient fields, which are not always clearly visible to the untrained eye but show up as low banks of earth and stone and lines of large stones. Odd changes in the lie of the land provide another clue: these were originally cultivation terraces.

The best place to look out for this old field pattern is in the dry valley running east from The Wick, as the boundaries are aligned up and down the slope on the northern flank. I was also intrigued by the Wick Stream, with its seven ancient stone dams, six of which are in more or less their original state. They would have split the stream into a series of pools, which could have been used for watering cattle or conserving water in dry weather. Another theory is that the damming of the Wick Stream enabled these Iron Age farmers to grind corn by means of the small horizontal water wheels in 'click mills'.

Apart from fields and dams, there are the outlines of the huts where they lived. The climate would have been similar to our own, with warm, damp summers and mild winters. They probably had ox-drawn ploughs, and not long ago a stone ploughshare was found near East Pond. Cattle and sheep were kept, as well as goats, pigs, hens and geese. The author of the archaeological guide, J G Evans, believes that the Skomer settlement was probably typical of its time in western Britain, but is practically unique in the richness of its remains.

Did those hard-working people of long ago admire the scenery, or take it for granted? In its essentials it was much the same as today, with the

Enclosures are common, exclosures pretty rare. This one is on Skomer Island, and the idea is to keep rabbits out to see what happens to the vegetation when it isn't being ceaselessly nibbled away.

long Atlantic rollers breaking white at the base of towering cliffs, and Ramsey Island like a beached whale across the broad sweep of St Brides Bay. Skomer is a green table raised high above the sea, its grass cropped short by the nibbling of rabbits. What would the island be like without their ceaseless foraging? For the answer we turn to a Skomer speciality – the rabbit exclosure. There are several on the island, the largest at Pigstone Bay. This was fenced off in 1973 and the vegetation allowed to grow freely. The result is a dense mass of greenery which looks curiously unattractive beside the Skomer we know. I was struck by the absence of colour, as the dense fescue grass clearly chokes off many of the flowers we find outside this botanical ghetto. There's clearly something to be said for the humble rabbit.

Another point of interest is the old farmhouse in the middle of the island. It dates from 1843, when Skomer was being extensively farmed and its produce exported. The only building still in use is the cowshed, which has now been converted into accommodation for visitors, but you can wander into the farmyard and see an old Fordson tractor rusting away and, in the shelter of a wall, the only tree to be found on Skomer – a black poplar.

What can one say about the cliff scenery of Skomer that doesn't exhaust already weary adjectives? It is always spectacular; worth a million of anyone's money. The seascapes are marvellous, the views in all directions exciting. And, for the geologically minded, there are the rocks to interpret – they form part of the Skomer Volcanic Group, which extends from Grassholm in the west to the Marloes peninsula and St Ishmaels in the east. The outcrops of whitish rock were once lava flows and the shale between, covered with vegetation, was originally ash.

Throughout the season there are regular trips to Skomer and Skokholm from St Martin's Haven, and to Caldey from Tenby. Caldey has its community of monks, who farm the island and make perfume out of gorse and lavender. They aren't the only inhabitants, as a number of families live on the island and in summer there could be as many as 2,000 day trippers. Caldey has considerable charm and some find it Mediterranean in atmosphere, with its white-walled monastery and beautiful flower gardens. There are cliff walks and sandy beaches and, for the historically minded, a stone with both ogham and Latin script at the old priory church, with its Norman

The old tractor's 'dead' but won't lie down ... It reminds us that cultivation of the unpromising soil of Skomer continued until fairly recent times.

tower and leaning spire. One authority has it that the stone may well have been a pagan monument which was Christianized by an evangelist who chiselled away some of the heathen lines and put in their place the script which, translated, reads: 'And I have fashioned the sign of the Cross upon it. I pray all who return to the mainland to make fervent prayer for the soul of me, Catuoconus.'

Christian or Moslem, atheist or agnostic, these off-shore islands are among the most distinctive delights of the Pembrokeshire Coast National Park. They emphasize the fact that this is a park in which the sea is the dominant influence; constantly changing, forever pounding the rocks or stretching long white fingers up smooth reaches of sand, never more than a few miles distant wherever you may be.

7 **Path of sheer pleasure**

The Pembrokeshire Coast Path stretches for 180 miles, which is roughly the distance from London to Chester. Some claim to have walked the entire length in three and a half days, but this is beyond the endurance – or the inclination – of most visitors. Ten to fourteen days would be a more reasonable time to allow yourself to cover the distance, but of course you don't have to contemplate such a marathon at all; the path is there to enjoy, in whole or in part, and is intended as a pleasure rather than a physical punishment.

It's important to remember that the path didn't spring up overnight, as a kind of gift of nature. It took seventeen years to establish, after the idea was approved in 1953. A great deal of diplomacy was required – and determination. In his excellent guide, *The Pembrokeshire Coast Path*, John H Barrett recalls:

'The great majority of the landowners approached in Pembrokeshire were reasonable and even generous in their approach to the path and quickly signed footpath dedications where new rights-of-way were required. Eventually there remained only a hard core of objectors who used every legal and administrative device to postpone the day on which strangers might walk the rough edge of the cliffs round their land – in most cases a rough edge so overgrown with gorse and blackthorn that the owner had no possible alternative use for it. . . .
When in due course the line was legally established, the problems of making a passable path arose. . . . Thickets of gorse and bramble, steep screes, boggy bottoms, long lengths remote from even a small lane were only some of the problems which confronted an entirely inadequate manpower. In some stretches a mini-bulldozer was used and those who walk the path will find it incredible that a piece of machinery could have been manœuvred over such terrain. Field banks have been straddled by oak stiles and heavy baulks shifted to bridge streams.'

Other detailed guides to the coast path are also available, and are listed in our bibliography. Here I shall merely list some of the points of interest, starting in the south and working our way round to the north.

At Amroth, the blackened, matted remains of a 7,000-year-old forest are revealed at low tide. There are fine views over Carmarthen Bay on the way to Wiseman's Bridge. At Saundersfoot, the shingle beach has pebbles which were originally part of ballast dumped by ships loading coal there last century.

Monkstone Point has views of Gower, Lundy Island and the Black Mountains; just south of it, note the wave-cut platform beneath black shales and ginger sandstones.

South-west of Tenby, there are caves and blowholes between Giltar Point and Lydstep Haven, where in days of sail sloops loaded limestone for Bideford and Cardigan.

At Priest's Nose, the headland on the southern side of Manorbier Bay, the King's Quoit burial chamber stands alongside the coast path. Manorbier Castle, which Leland called 'the most perfect model of an old Norman baron's residence', is well worth a visit.

Swanlake Bay, with its sandy beach, is off the beaten track; Freshwater East decidedly on it. Its

The farmer does not deliberately create beauty, but we can see here how the differing uses to which fields are put add contrast and colour to the landscape. Here we are on the St David's peninsula, looking north over Whitesand Bay to Carn Llidi.

popularity led to some ghastly 'development' in the days when there was little control over such matters; the Park Authority is now doing its best to put things right.

At Greenala Point, the path cuts through the ramparts of an Iron Age fort. More recent history comes to mind at Stackpole Quay; it was the place where provisions arrived for the powerful Cawdors, who in the eighteenth century held the 15,000-acre Stackpole Estate. There's a short, delightful walk along the coast path from Stackpole Quay to Barafundle Bay.

Broad Haven South has a superb stretch of sands; a short detour takes one to Bosherston lily ponds. West of St Govan's Head is the tiny chapel of St Govan's, at the foot of the cliffs, and half a mile farther on the path passes Huntsman's Leap, a fearsome chasm 130 feet deep.

By way of Buckspool Down, Crickmail Down and Longstone Down we reach the famous bird colonies of Stack Rocks, with their guillemots, razorbills, kittiwakes, shags and fulmars. The car park here has a viewing platform above the Green Bridge of Wales, a freak rock formation caused by the joining

The vast expanse of golden sands at Freshwater West are always inviting, but those Atlantic rollers must always be treated with caution: bathing is dangerous here, due to a vicious undertow.

The seaweed drying hut at Freshwater West. At one time the gathering of edible seaweed, which was turned into the delicacy known as laverbread, was a flourishing local industry. This hut, which has been restored, is now the only one remaining.

of two caves which were on opposite sides of an old headland.

At Freshwater West, the rolling dunes served as the 'desert' location for Alan Ladd's heroics in the film *Red Beret* – but the beach is dangerous for bathers, due to quicksands and a vicious undertow. Don't miss the seaweed drying hut, which has been restored by the National Park. It reminds us that we are in a part of Wales where laverbread is eaten with relish. This greeny-black substance, which goes well with bacon, is made from edible seaweed which women used to gather here; at the turn of the century there were twenty huts like this on the headland.

Off the tip of the Angle peninsula is Thorn Island, with a Victorian fort – one of Palmerston's Follies – now used as an hotel. In the attractive village of Angle, look out for the ivy-clad ruins of a fourteenth-century fortified tower-house, a type of building peculiar to Pembrokeshire. This windswept peninsula, almost devoid of trees, has a charm all its own, and many of the fields on the hillsides preserve the shapes of medieval strip fields.

From ancient to modern; on its way to Pembroke the coast path skirts the huge Texaco refinery. This is the most populated part of Pembrokeshire, with Pembroke, Pembroke Dock, Neyland and Milford Haven all close together.

West of Milford, a ghostly tale may tempt one to make a short detour to the village of Herbrandston (pronounced Harborston by the locals). The shape

The Lagoon offers the delights of seclusion to those who cross the Angle peninsula to West Angle Bay, which looks out to the old Victorian fort on Thorn Island.

of a dagger is said to appear from time to time on the churchyard tombstone of Lieutenant Philip Carrol Walker, of the Royal Artillery, killed in a pub brawl in 1875.

Great Castle Head commands a fine view of Dale Roads and the Haven in general; from here two more Victorian forts are visible, on Stack Rock and at South Hook, across the water.

There are some handsome houses in Dale, a centre for sailing and surfing. Dale Fort – bearing the date 1856 – now houses the Dale Fort Field Centre, which specializes in marine biology but runs courses in other subjects too.

On the way to St Ann's Head the path skirts Mill Bay, where at sunset on 7 August 1485 Henry Tudor landed to greet his followers and begin the long march to Bosworth.

On the far side of the Head, the path offers exhilarating seascapes as the Atlantic rollers surge in; Frenchman's Bay gives way to Welshman's Bay before we reach the fine sweep of Marloes Sands. Here we find the Three Chimneys, an apt name for bands of Silurian sandstone and mudstone which have been forced up into vertical positions.

Gateholm Island can be reached by foot at low tide, but do be careful. At the Deer Park, on the tip of the Marloes peninsula, the path skirts Martin's Haven, where there are boat trips to Skomer and Skokholm in the season. At St Bride's Haven, stone coffins protrude from the eroded cliff; they are between 900 and 1,500 years old. An old rhyme goes:

> 'When the chapel as salting house was made
> Then St Bride's lost the herring trade'

which points a lesson of a kind. And so to Broad Haven, where a sphinx-like rock overlooks the splendid beach. The geologically minded will spot some good examples of folding, sea stacks and natural arches at the northern end of the beach, and there are well-defined caves at Madoc's Haven. Along this stretch of coast, we can see how the hard sandstone has stood up to the constant battering of the sea to form headlands, whereas little bays have been cut out of the softer shale.

The vast expanse of Newgale Sands is fringed by a huge storm beach of rounded pebbles, and as the path skirts the north shore of St Brides Bay it brings us to Solva, a delightful coastal village which seems ready-made for an artists' colony. There's an old lifeboat house on the quay but no longer a lifeboat, and wooded hills on either side.

On the way to St David's, an earthbank above the cove of Ogof y Ffos marks the end of Ffos-y-Mynach (Monk's Dyke), which crosses Dowrog Common on its way north to reach the sea west of Penberi.

Just over two miles further on, the path passes St Non's Chapel, reputedly the birthplace of St David's mother, Non; a short detour here takes one into St David's itself, which looks no more than a village but boasts a City Hall!

This section of coastline at Solva clearly illustrates how the harder rocks have stood up to the sea's onslaught to form headlands, whereas little inlets and bays have been carved out of softer shales.

The walk around St David's Head is sheer delight, and poses no great difficulty even for the less energetic. The tiny harbour of Porthclais, which has a car park, was importing timber from Ireland in Tudor times and exporting wheat and barley to Bristol.

St Justinian's – which can be reached by road from St David's – has a lifeboat house and the ruins of a little medieval chapel dedicated to Justinian, a man whose saintly ways were too much for his followers on Ramsey Island, who rebelled and cut off his head. Nothing daunted, Justinian is said to have promptly picked it up and brought it ashore. This is a good place for seal-spotting, and there are trips to and around Ramsey Island, which is less than a mile off-shore at this point.

At Whitesand Bay – a fine surfing beach where the Atlantic rollers thunder – look behind the dunes for the site of a chapel dedicated to St Patrick, who is said to have stood there looking across to Ireland, where destiny was to lead him. There are views of the Bishops and Clerks rocks, and the path then cuts across the magnificent St David's Head, with its hut circles and ditches.

Abereiddy has its famous Blue Lagoon, which is in fact a flooded quarry. Look out for traces of the tramroad which took the slates to Porthgain, where there's an eighteenth-century pub – the Sloop Inn – and an interesting row of old cottages.

Abercastle, still used by local fishermen, was a busy little port in sailing days; it overlooks Cwm Badau, Valley of Boats. Two miles on the path passes Aber Bach, where an old man is once said to have captured a mermaid.

Hard to believe, now, that Abercastle was once a busy little port where cargoes of limestone and coal were unloaded. Today it's given over simply to pleasure – and in this idyllic setting, there's no shortage of that.

The Blue Lagoon at Abereiddy was formed by accident, when an old quarry was flooded. This quiet beauty spot was once a thriving slate quarrying centre.

A memorial stone to the poet Dewi Emrys overlooks Pwll Deri, a place of wild beauty where even a poet's heart may find peace. Choughs and fulmars breed on these high, rugged cliffs, which culminate in Strumble Head, with its trim white lighthouse.

Two miles beyond Fishguard we reach the charming little beach of Pwllgwaelod, where the Sailors Safety Inn is sheer delight with its lobster pots, fishing nets, ship's bell and wheel; the dartboard is set in a lifebelt!

Needle Rock, off Dinas Head, is a breeding ground for great black-backed gulls, herring gulls, razorbills and feral pigeons; the Silurian grits have stoutly resisted wave erosion. And so to the handsome little town of Newport, with its castle – privately owned – and Georgian houses. In the nineteenth century, there were shipyards at The Parrog, turning out square-rigged vessels and schooners.

The clifftop walk between Newport and Ceibwr Bay is hard going for inexperienced walkers, but those who take steep gradients in their stride are rewarded with superb seascapes.

Four miles on from Ceibwr Bay we reach Cemaes Head, a fine viewpoint where we look across Cardigan Bay as far as Bardsey Island on a clear day. From here the path descends to the smooth sands of Poppit, to reach journey's end at St Dogmael's. Happy walking!

8 The challenge of success

Running a national park is not simply a question of letting the grass grow and making sure the sea birds have space enough to lay their eggs in; it is a complex task requiring diplomacy as well as determination.

The National Park Authority, like its counterparts in the other national parks of England and Wales, has been charged by Parliament with two main duties: to preserve the natural beauty of the area and to promote its enjoyment by the public. There is, however, a third consideration: the welfare of the local community. The park, after all, is not a place simply set aside for recreation, but a part of Wales where people live out their lives and have the same expectations as those who come here to recharge their batteries. The Park Authority has gone on record as saying that it 'regards the social and economic well-being of local residents as a policy objective' within the context of its statutory obligations. Happily, beauty often goes hand-in-hand with economic well-being, and indeed an attractive, accessible national park is good for tourism. The Authority's encouragement of crafts such as pottery, weaving, woodwork, leatherwork, slate carving, glass blowing and glass engraving is a case in point. The existence of these workshops

Newport provides all the pleasures of small-town living – the corner shop is an essential part of life, and a friendly chat makes the wheels of business turn all the more smoothly.

not only adds to the prosperity of the community, but makes the area more attractive for visitors. The Authority has also joined in co-operative ventures which have preserved historic sites and, at the same time, been of direct benefit to people living around them. A prime example of this is at Porthgain, where a united effort between the Park Authority and local interest resulted in the purchase of the picturesque harbour – a monument to Pembrokeshire's industrial past – and the old terraced cottages known as the Street. The cottages, previously tenanted, are now owner-occupied, and the harbour is in the safe hands of the Park Authority. Another joint venture of this kind was at Nevern, where the authority helped the community council to buy Nevern Castle.

The most obvious conflict between economic well-being and conservation – or, put more bluntly, between brass and beauty – has been in the oil industry's encroachments along the shores of Milford Haven. There's no doubt that the Pembrokeshire Coast National Park suffered a serious challenge when, within five years of its inception, the Government announced that Milford Haven was to be developed as a major oil port. The economic argument was overwhelming: in 1957 the potential of the North Sea had not yet been realized, and it seemed that Britain's industrial future depended on vast quantities of oil being brought from the Persian Gulf in huge tankers – or, as they increasingly came to be known, supertankers. For many people, however, it seemed depressing proof that when the chips were down, governments placed no great store on the preservation of the countryside. National parks are not the place to locate large-scale industrial developments. John Dower defined a national park as 'an extensive area of beautiful and relatively wild country in which . . . the characteristic landscape beauty is strictly preserved'. Opinions vary on the visual damage done by the refineries and their related buildings. In spite of the landscaping and colouring schemes embarked upon by the oil companies, there is no hiding them. They are, however, confined to a small area, and in effect have meant an extension of the urban development in what was already the most populated part of Pembrokeshire. It is also a fact that many people enjoy watching the tankers in the Haven. Midway through the 1980s, however, the arguments were beginning to seem posthumous. Through careful planning control the park had survived the assault, and the oil industry's operations had substantially contracted.

It was still possible, however, that a new threat might come from the search for oil and gas in the Celtic Sea – a search which had been spasmodic since the first flurry of activity in the 1970s. The Park Authority was adamant that it would resist the establishment of any major landfall site along the coast for the treatment of oil or gas pumped ashore. This, in its view, would be visually disastrous. It was also keeping a wary eye open for plans to exploit the coal reserves of Pembrokeshire by means of open-cast mining: any proposals to have this in the park itself are likely to be fiercely resisted.

Oil pollution is a constant fear. In 1978 the Greek tanker *Christos Bitas* ran on to the Hats and Barrels rocks in a flat autumnal calm and 2,000 tons of oil spilled out. Fortunately it could be effectively sprayed and very little of it came ashore. There was a more serious incident in 1985, when the small coastal tanker *Bridgeness* ran on to the same rocks while going from Milford to Ireland. More than 200 tons of heavy fuel oil spilled out, and mixed with the much lighter gas oil the vessel was carrying to spread out thinly over a wide area. It happened in the middle of the breeding season and at least 5,000 sea birds were killed, although no oil came ashore. Whenever an oil spillage occurs action to combat it is swift, as there are contingency plans to deal with a variety of situations. These have been drawn up by Dyfed County Council, in association with the National Park Authority. In addition, research into the ecological effects of oil pollution is carried out in the Orielton Field Studies Centre, near Pembroke. Prevention, however, is better than cure, and at the time of writing pressure was being put on the government to keep the area between Grassholm and the Smalls free from cargo ships.

Some problems arise from the very popularity of the Pembrokeshire Coast National Park, many of them similar to problems encountered in other parts of the countryside. Small-scale erosion occurs through over-use along certain sections of the coast, and sand-dune systems are especially at risk. However, the National Park Authority is responsible for the maintenance of footpaths and undertakes schemes which will protect fragile habitats such as sand dunes. Moreover, not every visitor is familiar with the country code, although the Park's information service helps to remind people about it. Gates are left open and people have even been known to picnic blithely in fields of young corn, exclaiming when reprimanded. 'This can't be corn – it's green – corn is yellow, isn't it?' It is also frequently assumed that all the land in a national park must, of necessity, be publicly owned. In fact, designation of a region does not affect property ownership in the slightest, and most of the land in the Pembrokeshire Coast National Park remains in private hands. Another perennial problem is that of litter, which is not only unsightly but a danger to livestock; a piece of metal, glass or plastic carelessly thrown away can mean injury or even death. It is no solution, either, to bury litter in the sand; chances are that the next tide will leave it exposed.

It used to be fashionable to speak disdainfully of the 'rash' of caravan sites along the south Pembrokeshire coast, but the Park Authority has come to grips with the problem and uncontrolled development of this kind is now a thing of the past. The number of pitches for static and touring caravans has been stablilized for some years, and sites which were regarded as particularly offensive to the eye have been removed altogether. This has been achieved either by buying a site simply to

There can be few more agreeably sited caravan sites than this one at Lydstep Haven. One of the prime tasks of the National Park Authority has been the maintenance of high standards on these sites, and tight controls on the locations and numbers of caravans in the park.

A National Park viewpoint near Newport, set in exquisite countryside. Beauty like this can be preserved only if the community at large has the will to prevent its despoilation.

close it, or by practising the gentle art of persuasion – supported by the inducement of an alternative site, complete with planning consent, somewhere else.

The idea, though, is not to drive people away from Pembrokeshire; indeed, the National Park Authority positively welcomes those who come and aims to enhance their enjoyment of the park with information services and programmes of guided walks and special exhibitions. The number of visitors to the park was approaching a million and a quarter a year by the mid-1980s and was expected to expand by twenty-five per cent by the end of the decade. The overwhelming majority of these were people who came to stay for a week or two rather than on a flying visit, and it has been calculated that for every day tripper there are seventy holidaymakers. The coastal strip around Tenby and Saundersfoot is still the most popular destination, and the St David's peninsula and St Brides Bay are other favourite areas, but the northern section of the park and the Daugleddau region, with its lovely river scenery, are curiously by-passed by many visitors. New footpaths have been opened up in the Daugleddau in the hope that its quiet delights will be better appreciated in future. There are also plans to make the Milford Haven area more attractive, with a wider range of accommodation and the opening of marinas – developments which involve co-operation between the Park Authority, district councils, the Wales Tourist Board and the Welsh Development Agency. Apart from benefiting visitors, a healthier economy would be a boon to an

Tree planting and clearing on the Stackpole Estate – the kind of routine country tasks that townspeople often take for granted. Visitors alive to such things increase tenfold their enjoyment of a holiday.

area which has the worst employment record in Pembrokeshire.

Farm holidays are increasingly popular, and their growth is an intriguing example of the way the two major industries of Pembrokeshire, agriculture and tourism, are inextricably entwined. The ideals of the national park have been cheerfully accepted by the vast majority of farmers, who work hand-in-glove with the Park's wardens and rangers. The Park Authority helps farmers by waymarking footpaths and giving them grants for landscape conservation work such as tree planting. There's no denying, however, that some aspects of modern farming work against the interests of conservation. The improvement of land can mean the destruction of important habitats, such as moorland, heath and wetlands. The Park Authority can step in to prevent grants being made for this work, but wherever possible it settles the issue amicably, sometimes entering into management agreements with individual farmers and paying compensation for any loss they might incur by not going ahead with their plans.

Another difficulty is that many prehistoric sites stand on farmland, and are threatened by ploughing as well as trampling by livestock. Some were protected in the past by being incorporated into fieldbanks, but fields are larger today and hedges fewer. Here again co-operation is vital, and farmers with scheduled sites on their land often receive 'acknowledgement' payments from the Department of Environment, on the understanding that they keep it free from scrub and do nothing to damage it. Remember, though, that apart from the 176 sites in the park scheduled as ancient monuments there are more than 100 unscheduled sites which are deemed to be of archaeological importance!

More than 6,000 acres of land in the park are held by the military, most of it given over to the tank firing ranges at Castlemartin. This is fiercely resented by many people, who see no place in a national park for activity of this kind. Indeed, the Countryside Commission maintains that military training is incompatible with national park purposes, and will assist the National Park Authority in resisting any demands for an increase in military landholding. In Pembrokeshire itself, however, there are even conservationists who point out that the soldiers were there long before the park was set up, and that the special character of this open landscape has, in a way, been preserved by the military: if it hadn't been set aside for these exercises, it would probably have been covered with wheat and barley by now. This is, in fact, the largest area of unimproved lowland grassland in Wales, roughly ten square miles in size. It has never been sprayed with insecticides, and provides a very broad habitat for a variety of birds which are unable to breed in such numbers elsewhere. It's a roosting place for waders, and other species to be found there include wheatear, chough, reed bunting, meadow pipit and peregrine falcon. The land has practical use for farmers as well; cattle and sheep from the Preseli Hills spend the winter in this milder climate. All the year round, some parts of the area are open to the public when the military isn't actually using it: look out for press announcements and notices along access roads, or contact National Park information centres.

The more one studies the complex nature of a national park, the more one is driven to the conclusion that a Park Authority has to combine the wisdom of Solomon with the realpolitik of a Bismarck. It must cling to its ideals, yet never live in cloud-cuckoo-land.

The achievements of the Pembrokeshire Coast National Park are difficult to summarize. There is the creation of the Pembrokeshire Coast Path, which brings so much joy to so many; the land reclamation

Peace, perfect peace . . . a scene at Nolton Haven which captures the sense of ease and tranquillity one finds in a National Park.

schemes which have swept away concrete pillboxes and other ugly wartime relics; the stringent curbs on unsightly caravan sites; the countless initiatives, such as the leasing of Carew Castle, the acquisition of woodland and the kind of co-operation which has given the public free access to the unique grounds of Upton Castle. And there is the way people have been made aware of the richness and diversity of this corner of Wales. The guided walks and talks are immensely popular, and the purpose-built Broad Haven Information Centre is a model of its kind. Not least, there is the way the Park Authority has won the enthusiastic support of the community. The value of this should not be underestimated; it shows itself in the warmth of the welcome that's extended to everyone who steps over the threshold of the Land of Mystery and Magic.

Selected places of interest

The numbers after each place-name are the map grid references to help readers locate the places mentioned. Ordnance Survey maps include instructions in the use of these references.

Ordnance Survey Landranger maps for Cardigan (145), St David's and Haverfordwest (157) and Tenby (158) cover the national park.

ABEREIDDY (SM 796310) Once-thriving slate centre noted for Blue Lagoon, fortuitously created by the flooding of an old quarry.

ABER MAWR (SM 882345) Sandy beach at end of Pen Caer peninsula.

AMROTH (SN 163072) Southern end of coastal path; low tides reveal remains of prehistoric forest.

BARAFUNDLE (SR 992950) Superb beach easily reached on coast path from Stackpole Quay.

BEDD MORRIS (SN 037365) Standing stone on moorland.

BLACKPOOL MILL (SN 060145) Renovated corn mill in beautiful setting.

BOSHERSTON POOLS (SR 970946) Lovely walks past man-made pools famous for their waterlilies.

BROAD HAVEN (SM 860125) Marvellous expanse of sand and National Park Information Centre specializing in marine life.

BROAD HAVEN SOUTH (SR 978942) Fine sandy beach fringed by dunes.

CALDEY ISLAND ABBEY (SS 142966) Monastic tradition upheld by Cistercians who farm the island and make perfume.

CAREW (SN 045037) Splendid castle with Elizabethan façade, in lyrical setting. French Mill nearby is only surviving tidal mill in Wales. Stone cross in village dates from c.1035.

CARNALW (SN 139337) Preseli tor with frost-shattered blocks and rare example of chevaux-de-frise.

CARNINGLI (SN 062372) Spectacular hillfort with enclosures and hut sites.

CARN LLIDI (SM 738280) Fine viewpoint; Snowdonia and Ireland may be seen on clear days.

CARNMENYN (SN 144326) Source of bluestones (spotted dolerite) of Stonehenge.

CARREG SAMSON (SM 848335) Popular name for longhouse dolmen.

CARREGWASTAD (SM 927406) French troops came ashore here in 1797 in 'last invasion of Britain

CASTELL HENLLYS (SN 117390) Replica of Iron Age round house.

CASTLEMARTIN (SR 915984) Rare example of medieval cattle pound.

CILGERRAN CASTLE (SN 196432) Romantic ruins, much loved by landscape painters, overlooking River Teifi.

CLAWDD-Y-MILWYR (or Warrior's Dyke) (SM 723279) Iron Age promontory fort with circular hut sites.

CLEGYR-BOIA (SM 737251) Stone Age site named after Irish freebooter.

DALE FORT (SM 825051) Victorian fort housing Field Studies Council Centre, near seaside village noted for sailing and surfing.

DOWROG COMMON (SM 775270) Sedgy furze moor rich in plant and bird life – buzzard, curlew, lapwing, snipe and other species.

FISHGUARD (SM 958370) Peace treaty with invading French was signed at Royal Oak pub; Lower Town became mythical 'Llareggub' for film of *Under Milk Wood*.

FOEL CWMCERWYN (SN 094312) Summit of main Preseli ridge (1,760 ft; 537 m) above Pantmaenog Forest.

FOEL DRYGARN (SN 157336) Iron Age hillfort incorporating Bronze Age burial cairns.

FOEL ERYR (SN 065321) Rises to height of 1,535 ft (468 m) alongside Haverfordwest-Cardigan road; superb panorama, with viewfinder.

FRESHWATER EAST (SS 020980) Ever-popular beach where pre-war 'shackery' has given way to new holiday accommodation.

FRESHWATER WEST (SR 885990) Sandy beach (not for bathing) with dunes and hut where edible seaweed was dried before being made into laverbread.

THE GANN (SM 810070) Thriving wildlife habitat with Brent geese, goldeneye, red-breasted merganser and other species in winter.

GATEHOLM (SM 770072) Island accessible at low tide; barnacle geese in winter; site of Celtic monastic community.

GORS FAWR (SN 135295) Stone circle beneath Mynydd Preseli

GRASSHOLM (SM 598093) Outermost island with large gannet colony.

GREENALA FORT (SS 008964) Promontory fort with elaborate earthworks.

GREEN BRIDGE OF WALES (SR 925945) A geological freak not to be missed – a natural arch of majestic appearance jutting out from limestone cliffs.

GUPTON BURROWS (SR 890990) Dunes where further reclamation is opposed because of richness of flora.

GWAUN VALLEY (SN 005349) Beautiful wooded valley with abundant wildlife and prehistoric remains.

HAVERFORDWEST (SM 955155) Historic county town where Norman castle contains county museum; steep, narrow streets with Regency houses; old quays. National Park Information Centre.

KILGETTY (SN 126072) Former mining village with National Park Information Centre explaining area's industrial history.

KING'S QUOIT (SS 059973) Cromlech on headland near Manorbier.

LAMPHEY (SN 019009) Once-luxurious palace for bishops of St David's; well-stocked fishponds now marshy hollows.

LLANWNDA (SM 933395) Tiny village with bellcoted church typical of north Pembrokeshire.

LLAWHADEN (SM 074175) Remains of castle which protected estates of bishops of St David's.

LYDSTEP POINT (SS 094975) Superb limestone promontory above firm sands.

MANORBIER (SS 063978) 'The pleasantest spot in Wales' according to Giraldus Cambrensis, who was born in the beautifully sited castle. A twelfth-century church stands on the hill opposite.

MARLOES (SM 795084) Neat village with clock tower and nearby sands where vertical beds of rock have been named the Three Chimneys.

MARTIN'S HAVEN (SM 760092) Sheltered cove at Deer Park with boat trips to Skomer and Skokholm.

MILFORD HAVEN (SM 905058) Planned town on a gridiron pattern; fine views over the harbour from Hamilton Terrace. Nelson relics in St Katherine's Church.

MILL BAY (SM 808033) Henry Tudor landed here in 1485

MUSSELWICK (SM 785090) Firm sands backed by steep cliffs.

MYNACHLOG-DDU (SN 145305) Moorland hamlet below Mynydd Preseli, with memorial to poet Waldo Williams just to the west.

NEVERN (SN 083400) Hamlet in delightful setting. The Late Perpendicular church is approached along an avenue of yew trees, one of which is called the Bleeding Yew because of its blood-red sap. A sixth-century stone pillar inscribed in Latin and ogham stands near the intricately carved Nevern Cross. A motte-and-bailey castle overlooks the river.

NEWGALE (SM 847224) Two miles of sand backed by pebble embankment; traces of drowned forest at very low tide.

NEWPORT (SN 057392) Attractive small town with Norman castle (privately owned) and church with Norman font; firm sands and dunes. National Park Information Centre.

NEYLAND (SN 965051) Associations with Brunel – look out for Brunel Avenue and Great Eastern Terrace.

NOLTON HAVEN (SM 860186) Congregational Chapel (1858) built in classical style

PARC Y MEIRW (SN 998359) Stone alignment at roadside in Gwaun valley.

PEMBROKE (SM 983015) Ancient borough occupying a narrow ridge where Arnulph of Montgomery built 'a slender fortress of stakes and earth' in 1093. The present castle, begun about 1190, was the birthplace of the first Tudor king, Henry VII. The thirteenth-century St Mary's Church is nearby. Parts of the town wall remain. Park Information Centre.

PEMBROKE DOCK (SM 966034) Fine Martello towers at either end of the dockyard.

PEN CAER (SM 910400) Peninsula rich in archaeological remains.

PENTRE IFAN (SN 099370) Outstanding example of Neolithic cromlech, with huge capstone.

PICTON CASTLE (SN 011134) Privately owned but with access to gardens and Sutherland Gallery.

POPPIT SANDS (SN 155487) Extensive sandy beach at end of coast path.

PORTHGAIN (SM 814326) Once-busy harbour with relics of quarrying days; listed buildings where crushed stone was stored before export.

PWLL DERI (SM 893385) Haunt of grey seals; memorial to poet Dewi Emrys.

RAMSEY (SM 705235) Island off St David's Head with sea birds and seals; boat trips from St Justinian's.

ROCH CASTLE (SM 881212) Thirteenth-century Landsker castle perched high on a crag.

ROSEBUSH (SN 074293) Atmospheric remains of old quarries.

ST DAVID'S (SM 752252) Smallest city in Britain with cathedral in hollow; the present building was begun by the Norman bishop Peter de Leia about 1182. Bishop Gower built the splendid stone choir screen and the Bishop's Palace, with its elegant arcaded parapet, during the first half of the fourteenth century. The misereres were carved in the choir stalls in the fifteenth century, and the elaborately carved nave roof of grey Irish oak and the fan-vaulted ceiling of the Holy Trinity Chapel are of the sixteenth century. The ruins of St Non's Chapel, reached by a lane running south of St David's, are in a fine position overlooking St Non's Bay. St David is reputed to have been born on the spot in a thunderstorm; a nearby well, also named after his mother, Non, is said to have curative powers. Park Information Centre

ST GOVAN'S CHAPEL (SR 967929) Tiny chapel at foot of cliffs.

SAUNDERSFOOT (SN 137047) Popular resort where yacht-filled harbour has known sterner days, exporting coal last century.

SKOKHOLM (SM 735050) Sea birds and wild flowers galore; site of Britain's first bird observatory.

SKOMER (SM 725090) National nature reserve which is one of finest sea-bird colonies in Europe; seals, prehistoric fields and dams.

SKRINKLE HAVEN (SS 080973) Cliffs

of red marl and sandstone, laid down in Triassic times.

SOLVA (SM 805245) Exquisite coastal village with colourful harbour and old lime kilns.

STACK ROCKS OR ELEGUG STACKS (SR 930945) Massive limestone pillars where auks breed in great numbers.

STEPASIDE (SN 138077) Picturesque ruins of nineteenth-century iron-works.

STRUMBLE HEAD (SM 895415) Stupendous cliff scenery; lighthouse just off-shore.

TENBY (SN 134005) Charming resort with Georgian terraces. The fifteenth-century Tudor Merchant's House is now a museum. Fragmentary remains of thirteenth-century castle. St Mary's, also thirteenth-century, is the largest parish church in Wales, with elegant arcade. The town walls have round towers in places, and the barbican at the south gate has five arches. Sandy bays and Victorian fort on St Catherine's Rock. National Park Information Centre.

TREFEIDDAN MOOR (SM 733250) Haunt of garganey and red-breasted merganser in early spring.

TREFRÂN CLIFF COLLIERY (SM 858197) Traces of Victorian pit which had undersea workings.

TREGWYNT (SM 893338) Old woollen mill still producing traditional weaves.

UPTON CASTLE (SN 021047) Delightful wooded grounds with amazing variety of trees and shrubs.

WEST ANGLE BAY (SM 852032) Small bay with rock pools; views to Thorn Island, with Victorian fort.

WHITESAND BAY OR PORTH MAWR (SM 732268) Fine surfing beach that sometimes yields traces of submerged forest.

WISEMAN'S BRIDGE (SN 145060) Sandy beach where full-scale rehearsal of D-day landings was held in 1944.

Bibliography

Barrett, John H *The Pembrokeshire Coast Path*, HMSO, 1979

John, Brian *Pembrokeshire*, David and Charles, 1984

Jones, Anthony *Welsh Chapels*, National Museum of Wales, 1984

Knights, Peter *Birds of the Pembrokeshire Coast*, Pembrokeshire Coast National Park, 1979

Lockley, R M *Dream Island Days*, HF and G Witherby, n.d.

Lockley, R M *Pembrokeshire*, Robert Hale, n.d.

Miles, Dillwyn *Castles of Pembrokeshire*, Pembrokeshire Coast National Park, 1979

Miles, Dillwyn *Portrait of Pembrokeshire*, Robert Hale, 1984

Saunders, David *A Brief Guide to the Birds of Pembrokeshire*, H G Walters, 1976

Stark, Patrick *Walking the Pembrokeshire Coast Path*, H G Walters, 1980

Wright, Christopher John *A Guide to the Pembrokeshire Coast Path*, Constable, 1986

The Pembrokeshire Coast National Park has a range of publications, including area guides and subject guides, leaflets for young people, detailed walks and information on accommodation, beaches, boat trips, crafts, art galleries and studios, coastal scenery and so on. There is also a guide for disabled visitors and a leaflet on tours for the disabled.

Glossary

aber—confluence, river mouth
afon—river
allt—hill, slope, wood
arian—silver, money
arosfa—sheepwalk

bach—little, small
ban, pl. *bannau*—peak, crest, 'beacon'
banc—bank, hill, slope
bedd, pl. *beddau*—grave
bedwen, pl. *bedw*—birch
berllan, see *perllan*
betws—chapel-of-ease, oratory
blaen, pl. *blaenau*—head, end, source
bod—dwelling
bont—bridge
braich—arm, ridge
bren, see *pren*
brith—speckled
bro—region, vale
bron—hill-breast, hillside
bryn—hill
bugail, pl. *bugeiliaid*—shepherd
bwlch—pass
bychan, fem. *fechan*—little, lesser

cadair—seat
cadno—fox
cae, pl. *caeau*—field
caer, pl. *caerau*—fort, stronghold
calch—lime
cam—crooked
canol—middle
capel—chapel
carn, pl. *carnau*, *carnedd*—cairn, rock, mountain
carreg, pl. *cerrig*—stone, rock
castell—castle
cau—a hollow
cefn—ridge
celli—grove, copse

celynnen, pl. *celyn*—holly
cemais—river bends
ceunant—ravine, gorge, brook
cil, pl. *ciliau*—corner, retreat
cilfach—corner, nook
clawdd—hedge, ditch, dyke
clog, pl. *clogau*—crag, cliff
clun—meadow, brake
clydach—torrent
coch—red
coed—wood
collen—hazel
comin—common
corlan—sheepfold
corn—horn
cornel—corner
cors—bog
craig, pl. *creigiau*—rock
crib—crest, summit, ridge
croes—cross, cross-roads
crug, pl. *crugiau*—knoll, tump, cairn, hillock
cwar—quarry
cwm—valley, cirque
cwrt—court
cylch, pl. *cylchau*—circle
cymer, pl. *cymerau*—meeting of rivers

dan—under, below
dâr, pl. *deri*—oak
darren, see *tarren*
dau, fem. *dwy*—two
ddol, see *dôl*
deg, see *teg*
derwen, pl. *derw*—oak
dinas—fort
diserth—a retreat
disgwylfa—viewpoint
dôl, pl. *dolau*, *dolydd*—meadow
draw—yonder
dre, *dref*, see *tre*
du, fem. *ddu*—black

dulas—dark stream
dwfr, *dwr*—water
dyffryn—valley

eglwys—church
eira—snow
eithin—gorse
eos—nightingale
esgair—long ridge

fach, see *bach*
faen, see *maen*
fan, see *ban*
fawr, see *mawr*
fechan, see *bychan*
felin, see *melin*
ffald, pl. *ffaldau*—fold
ffawydden, pl. *ffawydd*—beech
ffin—boundary
ffordd—way, road
ffos—ditch
ffridd—mountain pasture
ffrwd, pl. *ffryddiau*—stream, torrent
ffynnon, pl. *ffynhonnau*—spring, well
foel, see *moel*
fron, see *bron*
fynydd, see *mynydd*

gadair (*gader*), see *cadair*
gallt—hillside (usually wooded)
gardd, pl. *gerddi*—garden
gam, see *cam*
garn, *garnedd*, see *carn*
garth—hill, height, enclosure
garw—rough, coarse
gelli, see *celli*
gilfach, see *cilfach*
glan—river bank, hillock
glas, *gleision*—green, blue, grey
gleisiad—young salmon
glyn—glen
goch, see *coch*
goetre—woodland dwelling
gors—bog
graig, see *craig*
grib, see *crib*
groes, see *croes*
gwaun, pl. *gweunydd*—moor, mountain pasture
gwernen, pl. *gwern*—alder, alder swamp

gwrach—witch, hag
gwyllt—wild
gwyn, fem. *gwen*—white
gwynt—wind
gwyntog—windy
gwyrlod—meadow

hafod, *hafoty*—summer dwelling
helygen, pl. *helyg*—willow
hen—old
hendre—winter dwelling, permanent home
heol, *hewl*—road
hir, pl. *hirion*—long

isaf, *isha*—lower, lowest

llan—church, enclosure
llannerch—clearing, glade
llech, pl. *llechau*—slab, stone, rock
llethr—slope
llety—small house, shelter
llwch, pl. *llychau*—lake
llwyd—grey, brown
llwyn—grove, bush
llyn—lake
llys—hall, court
llysiau—vegetables, herbs

maen, pl. *meini*—stone
maenol, *maenor*—chief's house, manor
maerdy—dairy
maes, pl. *meysydd*—field, plain
mawr—great, big
melin—mill
melindre—mill village
melyn—yellow
merthyr—church, burial place
mochyn, pl. *moch*—pig
moel—bare or bald hill
mynach—monk
mynydd, pl. *mynyddoedd*—mountain, moorland

nant, pl. *nentydd*—brook
neuadd—hall
newydd—new

odyn—kiln
oer—cold

ogof—cave
onnen, pl. *onn*, *ynn*—ash tree

pandy—fulling mill
pant, pl. *pantau*—hollow, valley
parc—park, field
pedwar, fem. *pedair*—four
pen—head, top, end
pennant—head of glen or valley
pentre—village, homestead
perfedd—middle
perllan—orchard
pistyll—spring, waterfall
plas—hall, mansion
pont—bridge
porth—gateway, entrance
pren—wood, wooden
pwll—pit, pool

rhaeadr, *rhaiadr*—waterfall
rhedyn—bracken, fern
rhiw—hill, slope, track up a slope, sloping track
rhos, pl. *rhosydd*—moorland
rhyd—ford

sain, *san*, *sant*, *saint*—saint
sarn, pl. *sarnau*—causeway, old road
sticill—stile
sych—dry

tafarn, pl. *tafarnau*—inn
tal—end
tan—end, below
tarren, pl. *tarenni*—rock-face, precipice

teg—fair, fine
tir—land, territory
tirion—sod, turf, country
tomen—mound
ton—grassland, ley
tor—break (of slope)
traeth—strand, beach, shore
trallwng—wet bottom land
traws—across, transverse, district
tre, *tref*—hamlet, home, town
tri, fem. *tair*—three
troed—foot
trum, pl. *trumau*—ridge
twrch—boar
twyn—hillock, knoll
ty, pl. *tai*—house
tyddyn—small farm or holding
tyle—hill, ascent, slope
tywarch—turf, peat, clod

un—one
uchaf—upper, higher, highest
uchel—high

waen, *waun*, see *gwaun*
wen, *wyn*, see *gwyn*
wern, see *gwern*
wrach (*gwrach*)—witch

y, *yr*, *'r*—the
ych, pl. *ychen*—ox
yn—in
ynys—island
ysgol—school
ystrad—valley-floor

Useful addresses

Pembrokeshire Coast National Park,
County Offices,
Haverfordwest,
Dyfed SA61 1QZ
(Tel. Haverfordwest (0437) 4591)

Council for National Parks,
45 Shelton Street,
London WC2H 9HJ
(Tel. 01 240 3603)

Countryside Commission
Office for Wales,
Ladywell House,
Newtown, Powys SY16 1RD
(Tel. Newtown (0686) 26799)

Dyfed Archaeological Trust,
Old Carmarthen Art College,
Church Lane,
Carmarthen
(Tel. Carmarthen (0267) 231667)

Field Studies Council
Orielton Field Centre, nr Pembroke
(Tel. Castlemartin (064681) 225)
Dale Fort Field Centre, Dale
(Tel. Dale (06465) 205)

HM Coastguard,
Maritime Rescue Sub-Centre,
Dale
(Tel. Dale (06465) 218)

The National Trust,
22 Alun Rd, Llandeilo
(Tel. Llandeilo (0558) 823476)

The Nature Conservancy Council,
Regional Officer,
Plas Gogerddan,
Aberystwyth
(Tel. Aberystwyth (0970) 828551)

Pembrokeshire Museums,
The Curator,
Scolton Manor,
nr Haverfordwest
(Tel. Clarbeston (043782) 328)

Preseli District Council,
Cambria House,
Haverfordwest
(Tel. Haverfordwest (0437) 4551)

South Pembrokeshire District
Council,
Llanion Park,
Pembroke Dock
(Tel. Pembroke (0646) 683122)

West Wales Trust for Nature
Conservation,
Market Street,
Haverfordwest
(Tel. Haverfordwest (0437) 5462)

Youth Hostels Association
In National Park Car Park,
Broad Haven
(Tel. Broad Haven (043783) 688)

Index

Page numbers in *italics* refer to illustrations.